Shipwrecked en route to Bombay and washed up on an exotic Eastern shore, Emily Hunter finds herself transplanted from Victorian England to a princely harem in India. How can she escape her luxurious prison where she has been brought for the pleasure of the ruler's son? Her only companions are the slave girls, her only hope the handsome Prince Dara himself. Emily's terror and suspicion of her captor, a man torn between his Eastern birthright and his Western education, culminate when the storm cloud of the Mutiny breaks over India. Yet even her own countrymen now regard Emily as an enemy. How can she survive, trapped between two violent worlds?

Fountains
of Paradise

Lee Stafford

MILLS & BOON LIMITED
London · Sydney · Toronto

First published in Great Britain 1979
by Mills & Boon Limited, 17–19 Foley Street,
London W1A 1DR

ISBN 0 263 73086 7

Filmset in VIP Plantin

*Made and printed in Great Britain by
C. Nicholls & Company Ltd.,
The Philips Park Press, Manchester*

CHAPTER
ONE

THE ship was a day or so away from Bombay, their destination, when the storm began in earnest. All day she had been ploughing through rough seas, but Emily, whose first crossing this was, had gritted her teeth and assumed that it was all perfectly natural, a part of the voyage which simply had to be endured.

During dinner, however, she noted that most of the other passengers had apparently kept to their cabins. The ship heaved violently from side to side, sending plates and decanters crashing, experienced stewards stumbled and fell, and seasoned travellers muttered that they had never experienced the likes of this, they were in for a really bad time. And her father, more than twenty years employed in the administration of the East India Company, who had made this crossing many times, was trying hard to conceal his anxiety.

It was absurd and somewhat ironic, Emily thought. Here was Edward Hunter, endeavouring to pretend, for his daughter's sake, that things were not so bad as they seemed, and here was the same daughter, doing her best to hide her fear from him, so as not to worry him, because she knew that in his heart, he wished she'd stayed safe in England.

Only as she was about to retire for the night did he abandon the pretence for a moment or two.

"Are you afraid, child?" he asked, pressing her hand tightly in his.

"A little," she confessed, for the dinner-time talk had impressed upon her that this was the exception, not the rule. "I'm going to try and sleep through it, and hope that by morning it will have blown itself out."

"That's the spirit," her father said encouragingly. "I shall try to do the same."

Six weeks prior to the night of that fateful storm, Emily's mother had been buried in the little churchyard at Overhampton, deep in rural Warwickshire. Drying her tears, Emily had looked up to the wide skies and permitted herself a sigh – of relief. The tears had been genuine. She had loved her Mama, although for as long as she could remember, she had been ailing, and the last year had been spent nursing her through her final, gruelling illness. But the relief was genuine, too, guilty though she felt to admit it. No more watching, in misery, the suffering she could do little to alleviate, no more the foetid smell of the sickroom, and now, the world beyond Overhampton, which prior to this day had lived only in her imagination, seemed to open wide before her. She, Emily Hunter, was eighteen years old, and free. Free!

It was the summer of 1856, and her father had arrived home on special leave, in time to be with his wife for those last days. Emily sensed that he shared her ambivalent emotions.

"My poor Christina," he said, after the funeral. "What kind of a husband have I been to her? All the years of our marriage, excepting those early ones, spent mostly apart, she here, I away in India."

"You had your work to do," Emily said comfortingly. She loved her father, although she had seen so little of him, and knew him only from his letters and his brief trips home on leave. It was a love born not of familiarity, but of an awareness of a kindred spirit. In some strange, unexplained way, they were alike.

"*You* understand that, don't you?" he said with a smile. "I don't have to explain to you why I could not leave India and the Company, and settle for some employment here, where I could be near her. I wish I could have made *her* understand why I stayed there."

It seemed perfectly logical to Emily that India had been her father's life and his calling. What she had never grasped was how her mother could bear not to be out there with him, and she said so, now, with a touch of bitterness.

He shook his head.

"No. You say that, but you don't know India, the climate, the harshness of it, the privations, in spite of all we take out there with us, all we surround ourselves with to cushion the shock. To live there demands a certain strength, and your mother was always delicate. She wilted like a flower before my eyes in the short time she spent there. And then, as you know, she lost the son that we had, dead of fever after only a few days, and she almost died herself. She never forgave India for taking her child, and when she knew you were to be born, she insisted on coming home. Somehow, the years passed, and she stayed on here. I accepted that she would never return. She was content, she had you, and was as well as she would ever be. It would have been cruel to force her to go back. I'm convinced it would quickly have killed her."

"But she would have been *with you*, for however short a time," Emily said fiercely, and he put a calm hand on her shoulder

"Emily, don't judge her too severely in your youthful romanticism. It wasn't purely selfish. She was afraid for you, too."

"There was no need. I have never ailed a day in my life," the girl said stoutly.

"No, and she thanked the mild, temperate English climate for that. You were precious to her, all she had left. And now . . ."

And now. The question hung in the air for several days before he could bring himself to voice it once more.

"What are we to do with you, Emily? There is this house and the money your mother left you, but you cannot live alone. We have no relatives in whose care you can be left until you are suitably settled."

Emily knew very well what that phrase "suitably settled" meant, for until illness deflected her from her purpose, her mother had made it clear that the only conceivable future for a well-brought-up young lady of Emily's class was matrimony, and the sooner the better. Emily, who had some odd ideas for a girl of her time, due perhaps to her voracious and often unsupervised reading, had resisted then, and resisted now.

"Married, you mean? Oh, Papa, must I be?"

"You know you must, Emily, eventually. What else is there for you to do?"

"Many things. Miss Nightingale was not married when she went out to Scutari to nurse the sick, for instance."

Her father was beginning to tire a little of this, she could see, although he answered patiently enough.

"Come now, you are not Florence Nightingale. You are eighteen, and marriage would be the best possible provision for your future. I have to ask you – is there anyone?"

She met his eyes with determination. "No one. If there were, if I loved, then of course it would be different. But this last twelve months I have been too busy looking after Mama, and our social life has been restricted. Before that I was introduced to young men, of course, but oh, Papa, they were all so dull and callow and . . . and ineffectual!" she burst out. "I could not bear to be married off to anyone like that. Please, Papa!"

"Hush, child. Don't excite yourself. You shall not be married to anyone you do not like, I promise you," he said soothingly. "But the Company will not extend my leave indefinitely, and we must decide, before I return, what is to be done with you. How would you like a year at a select academy for young ladies in Switzerland?"

"I should dislike it most intensely!" Emily said emphatically. "I have studied endlessly at home, for the enjoyment of it, and because there is little else to do, beyond calling on other ladies and leaving cards, and there is little your academy could teach me. I already speak French, Latin and Greek, I play the pianoforte passably, and sing, I paint and embroider and ride. And I've read more literature and poetry than their libraries could hold!"

"I see you are a very learned and accomplished young lady," he twinkled.

Emily clasped her hands and paced the room.

"It sounds horribly conceited, I know, and I did not mean it to. But school – oh, Papa!"

"No school then," he conceded. "I suppose it would only postpone the problem." And since he was a very liberal-minded father, for his day, he asked her, "What then, Emily? Tell me what you would like to do, short of joining Miss Nightingale."

This was the question she had been waiting for, and her reply was immediate, unhesitating.

"To go back to India with you. It's what I have always wanted," she said fervently, "ever since I was old enough to read your letters, although whilst Mama was alive, I knew it was not possible. I've read about the history and the customs, and you'd be surprised how much of the language I've learned, from the bits you've taught me when you've been home."

He put his head in his hands and rocked back and forth.

"Oh, Emily, you don't know what you are asking of me. Your mother scarcely in her grave, and you want me to take you to the one place she spent her life keeping you *from*. I can't do that, Emily."

"But Mama is dead, Papa," she pointed out. "Nothing we do can hurt her now."

He gave her a long, stern, thoughtful look. "Those are strange sentiments, child. Don't you believe your Mama can see you now?"

"No, I don't," she said boldly. "Take me to India, Papa. I can be your hostess, look after your home, entertain your guests. Oh, I know you have managed well enough all these years, but it will be different now. We shall get on splendidly, I know it. I shall be very useful to you, I promise."

He said, "Emily, Emily, you can have no idea what it is really like. No amount of reading can prepare you for the real impact of India, the assault upon all your senses, the effect upon your mind."

"You are trying to put me off, but you can't, because you love it so yourself," she said astutely. "Every time you come home, you are impatient to go back, as you are now. Why should I not love India, too? I am not like Mama. I'm strong, I'm never ill, and I'm not afraid. Mama is dead, but I'm alive, and I want this more than anything. I just know, somehow, that it's right for me, that it is what I was meant to do. Please, please take me with you."

He sighed heavily, and she sensed that he was beginning to weaken.

"It's a long journey out. I've seen men sicken, not to mention a slip of a girl like you."

"Yes, but women do go out there and make their homes, rear their families?" she persisted.

"Indeed, many do," he admitted.

"Then why shouldn't I go? You never know," she added slyly, "I might find a husband there. You are always saying how there are many eligible bachelors working for the Company, and a dearth of suitable brides."

At this he was obliged to laugh.

"Why, what a devious young woman you can be, when you are determined to have your way!" he exclaimed. "And I suppose there is a modicum of truth in what you say. India is a very good place in which to acquire a husband. Not that we should have any difficulty with you. You're as pretty as your Mama was when I married her."

His eyes grew serious again as he looked at his daughter. "Leave me alone for a while, Emily. I shall have to think most carefully about this."

She did as he asked, and did not press her advantage, and for the next few days India was not spoken of, but Emily's excitement grew into a positive fever of suspense. She could scarcely contain herself for longing to know what he had decided.

Finally, at the end of the week, he said with resignation, "Well, I daresay we must take you to London and buy you some new clothes."

She jumped up and flung her arms round his neck in a most indecorous display of delight, and when she had calmed down, he said soberly, "This is against my better judgment, Emily, you know that, don't you?"

She nodded. "I know, and I thank you, Papa. It will all go right, I promise."

He said, "We shall see. If there is any indication that the climate does not agree with you, or that the arrangement is not working, you shall be sent home forthwith. Is that understood?"

"Yes, Papa," she said, but her heart was a-flutter with excitement, and even his obvious reluctance could not dampen her enthusiam. She was going to India! Her life's dream was coming true.

From then on, events moved forward with alarming rapidity. The house was closed up, passages were booked – not the arduous route around the Cape, but the newer, fashionable way, to Alexandria by sea, then by land across Egypt, and thence by sea once more to Bombay.

Emily and her father travelled to London by train, in itself a new and exciting event for her, and there a maid was engaged to travel with her, and with the aid of the wife of one of her father's colleagues, clothes were fitted and made for her journey. There was a special type of corset, more suitable for the climate in which she was to be living, but although some concession was made to the heat in the way of somewhat lighter fabrics, Emily soon realised that she would be in no way less restricted by her clothing than she was in England. There would still be the cumbersome hoops of the crinoline, the tight stays and bodices, the frills and flounces of *mousseline de soie* and tarlatan, the camisoles, knickerbockers, shawls and mantles and petticoats. Being still in mourning for her mother, she was obliged to wear black, but some lighter colours were bought for the future, since who knew when she would be in London once more? The helpful and enthusiastic lady also ordered cases of cologne water, and even a pair of silver knitting needles, so that the moisture from the fingers at high temperatures should not rust the implements.

"You will find Bombay quiet and refined. Indeed, compared to Calcutta, for example, it is very sober," Emily was told. "There is little in the way of theatre, it is frowned on, and dances are infrequent."

Emily smiled. Having lived eighteen years in Overhampton, she was not afraid that Bombay would bore her.

Her father was more concerned about the possible ill-effects of taking his daughter out in the middle of the monsoon season. "I should have preferred to wait until November and let you have the cool weather first, but I have overstayed my leave, and must get back to my work as soon as possible."

"Will it be very hot?"

"Hot enough. The really hot weather is over by June. Now as it will soon be September, it will be raining a lot, but humid and unpleasant between the rains. However, it cannot be helped."

"I shall survive," she said philosophically, and indeed, she was determined to find something to like, even in the monsoon. And although the voyage to Alexandria, in an overcrowded French ship, was not exactly pleasant, she enjoyed the new sights and sounds at every port en route, the sojourn in Cairo at the comfortable oasis of Shepheards Hotel, the obligatory trips to see the Pyramids and the Sphinx.

But all this was nothing more than a prelude, an introduction to India, and she was thrilled when at last, after a rough, sixteen-hour journey to Suez by horse-drawn van, they finally embarked on the East India Company's comfortable, if not luxurious, steamer to Bombay. In Egypt, she had first heard the call of the East as it drew steadily nearer, and everything in her responded gladly to its call. And she saw, too, her father begin to relax, saw him begin to think – perhaps she will flourish.

All this flashed across her mind as she lay in her cabin, trying to sleep. Her newly-engaged maid had been too seasick to be of much help, and she had struggled out of her clothes and into her night-shift. The violence of the tropical storm increased; she heard the rain beating furiously on the decks, and the wind sighing, as she had never heard it before, a high-pitched, evil note. She buried her face in her pillow and strove to ignore the pitching of her bed, and after a while, she did drift off into a kind of dozing sleep.

She had no idea what time it was when she was roughly awakened. The bump she had heard in her sleep was her own body being tossed from its bunk. The cabin was pitch black, and she was lying on the floor, and through her confusion and terror, she was aware of something sinister – the steady note of the ship's engines, which had droned with them all the way from Suez, had changed to a helpless phut-phut. Then her stomach overturned as the ship seemed to do likewise, and she clung desperately to something, some article of furniture, she knew not what.

She heard screams and shouts of terror from the other passengers, and her father's voice crying out, "Emily! Emily! Where are you? Answer me, Emily!"

Through her fear, she had the sense to realise that in this darkness only her voice could guide him to her. She half shouted, half sobbed, "I'm here, Father – I'm here!" and a few moments later, she heard the cabin door burst open, heard him bumping and sliding and groping his way over to her, talking to her all the while, telling her to keep calm and he would help her, together they would make their way to the lifeboats.

After what seemed an age, he reached her side, his strong arms closed round her. She clung fiercely to him.

"Courage now, Emily," he said reassuringly. "Hold on to me and we shall get out of here. Don't waste your breath talking, now. We shall need all our strength and energy."

She grasped his hand more firmly to indicate that she understood, and together, they made their way, lurching and falling, grasping anything that would aid their progress, out of the cabin.

The decks were a dark, chaotic nightmare of screaming people and running feet, bodies bumping into each other in their frantic rush to save themselves. Any attempt to find her maid was hopeless. Edward Hunter grasped his daughter firmly round the waist, as he tried to get his bearings, and work out the quickest route to the lifeboats.

"Which way, Father?" she gasped.

He said, "I think –" and never finished the sentence, for in that moment, the doomed ship keeled over, the deck was no longer level beneath their feet, but almost vertical, and clinging helplessly to one another, they were swept overboard into the seething waves.

Water filled Emily's throat as her head went under; retching and spluttering, she broke the surface once more, dimly aware that her father's hand was still grasping her sodden nightdress. By good luck and presence of mind, Edward Hunter had managed to grasp a floating lifebelt, and he guided Emily's hands to it.

"Hold on!" he shouted, before the waves dragged them under again. "Don't let go!"

Emily clung on grimly, striving to hold her breath under the water, and draw deep gasps of air into her lungs each time she came up. She had no time to think of what had happened to the other passengers as the ship went down, there was nothing beyond the utter blackness of the night, the remorseless sea tossing them here and there like pieces of driftwood, and her raw, aching hands clinging to the belt. It was a night without end, she thought, a kind of hell.

The storm abated, but still father and daughter drifted, seemingly alone now on the empty sea. Emily felt herself beginning to sink towards a semiconscious state in which she thought she was dreaming. Her eyelids drooped, and her father's voice failed to rouse her from her increasing torpor. Once, she opened her eyes enough to see his white, strained face in the pale dawn just about to break, and heard him say, "Emily, for God's sake, you've got to hang on! Don't let yourself sleep, or it's the end."

"What does it matter?" she moaned. "We're going to die anyway, we're going to . . . just want to go to sleep. . . ."

Her eyes closed again, her head drooped on to the rim of the lifebelt. Her tired arms could no longer sustain the weight of her body against the drag of the water, and slowly her fingers loosened their hold, and began to slip.

She did not see her father untie the spotted neckerchief from around his neck, but dimly she seemed to feel him tying her wrists to the lifebelt. He too was worn out from their all-night struggle with the waves, and this action used up the last of his remaining resources of strength. Even if he could have summoned up the energy, the short neckerchief could never have served for both of them. Numb with fatigue as she was, she was brought back to alertness by the terrible realisation that he was deliberately forfeiting his hope of safety for hers. She had begged and pleaded for this trip to India, and it was going to cost him his life.

She tried to shout, "Father!" as in the light of the swiftly breaking dawn, she saw him drifting away from her, all this strength gone. But her voice only came out as a cracked whisper, and the expanse of sea between them widened. His last despairing cry of, "Emily – hold on!" faded away, and his white face became only a speck, bobbing on the waves. Then he was gone.

Emily's head sank down again on the lifebelt. Her heavy eyelids closed, and this time, she made no attempt to fight the inertia which claimed her. Her father was lost, and she had no will left to live. Slipping away into unconsciousness, her final thought was, this is it, the end, I am going to die . . . and she did not even care.

CHAPTER
TWO

SHE did not die, although she might well have done so, and been born again, so completely lost was the life she had lived all of her eighteen years until then. She woke as if from a dream, aware of sounds and sensations before she was able to open her eyes. There was a rocking motion beneath her, a dip and splash noise she could not identify, and the babble of male voices talking swiftly and argumentatively in a tongue she could not understand. She opened her eyes. She was lying on her back on the floor of a small boat, a fishing-boat most likely; there were bundles of nets all around her, and a strong stench of fish. The men were all dark-skinned and clad in white loin-cloths. They were rowing strongly and arguing among themselves, but they noticed she had come to, nudged each other and said, "Ah. . . ."

Their faces were curious but not unfriendly, and she was, in any event, too stupefied to be afraid. She felt very fragile and somehow disembodied, as if she were watching it all happen to someone else, and she knew, in some distant, still functioning region of her mind, that she must have presented an odd sight to them, lying there clad only in her long nightdress of white lawn, with her red-blonde hair in tangled disarray all around her no doubt equally white face.

They had reached the shore; the boat ground on the

shingle, and beneath that, there was the soft obbligato of waves trickling over sand and being sucked back again. The sky was brilliantly blue – making her head throb, tall palms waved languidly over a beach of incredible whiteness. The fishermen lifted Emily carefully out of the boat and carried her across the sand to a village of small, roughly-built huts, and inside the largest of these she was laid down gently on a bed of rush matting.

It was dim and cool inside the hut after the blinding sun and heat of the beach, and Emily could see little. She was given a little water to drink, which she took gratefully, and in a voice which felt like a croak to her, she said, "Please help. I am Emily Hunter . . . I am English . . . English. . . ."

The babble of argument swelled all around her once more, and she heard them repeating what she had said, with puzzlement, and then dawning comprehension. One of the men left the hut abruptly, and the rest watched her, talking in low, urgent tones among themselves. Very shortly another man arrived, a man wearing a long robe tied with a cummerbund around the waist. His appearance was totally different from the simple fishermen, and his voice, deeper and more authoritative, silenced theirs. She knew, without needing to be told, that this was the voice which was deciding her fate, but it seemed not to matter very much. Weak from fatigue and the after-effects of having been half drowned, she wanted to sleep and be left alone, and so she closed her eyes and let it all wash over her.

What followed was a nightmare of delirium, broken by occasional moments of sanity, so intermingled that she was never sure where one ended and the other began. She was aware of a swaying, rolling motion, as if she were back in the fishing-boat again, but there was no dip and splash of oars to indicate water, and she appeared to be in a bed with curtains around it; there were voices shouting orders, and then it all dissolved into chaos, there was only sweating and shivering, and terrible dreams.

How long this lasted she did not know, but finally the swaying stopped, gentle arms lifted her and set her down on something soft which did not move about. There were hushed female voices, and a cool, damp compress on her hot forehead. Then it was all gone once more, but this time the sleep was dreamless and healing. The awakening was all the worse, for she had her senses back; with blinding clarity she remembered the terror of the sinking ship, the awful night tossed about by the waves, and that dreadful moment when her father was carried helplessly away from her. She sat bolt upright and shouted, "Father!" It was a desperate shriek of grief and outrage.

Instantly, there was a flurry of silks, and she was surrounded by anxious young women in diaphanous gowns and tinkling jewellery. They were all dark and beautiful and spoke softly, and she could not understand one word of it. She could have wept for the Hindustani she had so painstakingly learned, for when she faltered a few halting words, she met only uncomprehending smiles, and patient nods of shining, elegant dark heads.

Emily looked despairingly around her. She appeared to be sitting on a divan in an alcove enclosed on three sides, and open on the fourth. It was night, for above her head a silver lamp burned, giving off a delicately sweet perfume whilst it illuminated a ceiling also inlaid with silver. The young women clustered all around;

some knelt, some stood, some sat on the edge of her bed. They smiled, and the air was full of their scent, and the rustle of their multi-coloured silks. From time to time, one or the other of them would reach out shyly to touch a strand of her golden hair. She was not yet to know it, but they had never before seen hair like hers. It was like a scene from a dream, yet she knew now that she was wide awake and sensible.

"I am Emily Hunter," she affirmed forcefully, as if the announcement of her identity could combat the growing sense of unreality about all this. "The ship went down, and I was rescued by fishermen. Who are you, and where am I?"

They looked at one another, spreading out their hands helplessly, and then suddenly, a large, fat, middle-aged matron with a wealth of double chins appeared, and miraculously the girls melted aside to permit her to come nearer. She laid her hand, surprisingly cool and competent, on Emily's forehead, and gave a murmur of approval, then she spoke to her, kindly but firmly.

Emily shook her head, demonstrating her lack of comprehension. Undismayed, the other woman clapped her hands loudly, and called, "Udepuri!"

There was the brisk shuffle of slippers on the marble floor, and then another girl appeared. A little older than Emily, perhaps in her mid-twenties, she was olive-skinned, dark of hair and eyes, and dressed as were all the others, but undoubtedly she was a European girl. The stout matron spoke to her in tones of authority, and she came closer to Emily, and said clearly in French, "I am bidden to ask if it is true that you are English, and if you are now feeling well."

They were, to Emily, the most beautiful words she had ever heard, simply because she understood them, because here was someone with whom she could communicate, who could explain for her the trance-like situation in which she found herself.

"I am well," she responded in French. "My name is Emily Hunter, and I am English. Please tell me where I am, and what happened to the rest of the people from the ship." Inside her, a fugitive hope still lived – she had been saved, might her father also have survived in the same manner?

A ripple of interest ran through the group beside her bed as she announced her nationality, and the French girl translated. The stout woman gave a smile of satisfaction, and responded volubly.

"*Bien.*" The girl named as Udepuri frowned a little with the effort of translation. "The person you see before you is called Qadir Bibi Bano. She is the Lady Protectress of the harem, the chief authority within its confines; she is here to help and counsel you in all things, and she is to be obeyed. As to your whereabouts, you are in the harem of Prince Murad, of the independent princely state of Bilkhondar."

The word "harem" jerked all Emily's senses into sharp awareness, for this was 1856, and she had not come out to the India of princes and harems, which she thought had all but passed into history, but to British India, of company officials and all the reassuring panoply of British administration; and furthermore, she had never even heard of Bilkhondar. Puzzled, she said, "But what am I doing here, and what of my father, and the ship?"

"I will ask," said Udepuri, and Emily listened anxiously as the reply came back to her.

"Qadir Bibi Bano asks me to tell you that the ship which brought you from across the sea was wrecked beyond recovery, and that according to the fishermen who picked you up in their boat, you were the sole survivor."

Emily covered her face with her hands and said brokenly, "Then my father must be dead."

"It must be so, *chérie*. I am sorry." They were all silent for a while, respecting her grief, then she withdrew her hands, sat up straight, and said with as much dignity as she could, "Then would you thank Qadir Bibi Bano for looking after me, and tell her that now I am quite recovered, I wish to see the representative of Her Majesty's Government."

The French girl did not trouble to translate this.

"You do not understand, *chérie*. There is no British government here, nor any representative of Britain. Bilkhondar is an independent, autonomous princely state. Prince Murad rules his own dominions, and his is the only law here."

"Then I have no business being here!" Emily cried, thoroughly alarmed. "Our ship was bound for Bombay, where I was going to live with my father, and that is where I should be. It will have been noted that the ship has not arrived, people will be expecting us. . . ."

"They will not be expecting you. Your ship, apparently, was many miles off course when it was lost, and even if they know what has happened to it, you will have been presumed drowned, along with the others. Bombay is very far from where you were rescued, and Bilkhondar is several days' journey inland, over the Ghats – the mountains. You were brought here in a litter, weak and only half-conscious."

She began to recall snatches of that swaying, nightmarish journey, and it only served to render her more deeply mystified. She had not been robbed – indeed, there had been nothing on her worth stealing – nor molested, and she had been brought here, seemingly with great difficulty, carefully tended and looked after. But why? It would have been easier to hand her over to the nearest form of British authority, and be done with her.

"I must leave here as soon as possible," she cried, in great agitation. "I must get to Bombay! I must!"

"No! You will never leave here. Do not even think of it," the French girl said. "Be warned by me, no one who enters these walls ever leaves. And your presence here is no accident. You were brought here deliberately, by design, and you will not be permitted to go."

"But why? Why?" Emily demanded, distraught, almost in tears.

By now, the Lady Protectress of the harem appeared to think their private conversation had gone on long enough, and she intervened, speaking reprovingly to the youthful interpreter, who said in a low voice, "I am bidden to speak only as directed. Later, if we can talk privately, I shall tell you what I know."

But Emily was in no state to be patient. Jumping to her feet, she pointed at Qadir Bibi Bano and shouted, almost hysterically, "Tell her! Tell her I must be sent back to my own people! At once!"

The older woman must have understood the gist of this from the desperation in the English girl's voice. She regarded her steadily, with dark, implacable eyes, then quite deliberately she raised her hand and struck Emily sharply across the face. Hysteria dissolved into tears, she threw herself on to the bed, face downwards, and wept fiercely. Not for the sake of the blow the Lady Protectress had dealt her, even though it was the first time in her life she had ever been hit in that fashion. That had merely broken the tension in her. She wept for her dead father, for the life that was gone, and the bright dream of the future which would now never be hers, and for the fear of the alien existence which now, inevitably, lay ahead of her.

She must have sobbed herself finally to sleep, for she awoke to the sound of the muezzin's voice. She was to hear it many times thereafter, but on this, the first occasion, she lay listening, drawn in spite of herself by the melodiously imperative Muslim call to prayer. And then, in the silence which followed, she heard them for the first time, the fountains, the sweet, refreshing murmur of water splashing into marble basins, the sound which would never again entirely leave her.

She opened her eyes to see the French girl seated at the foot of her bed. They were alone, and she held up her finger.

"Hush – speak quietly. I am commanded to tell Qadir Bibi Bano the moment you wake, so if you would talk, do not let them hear our voices," she whispered. "I am called Udepuri, but my given name was Simone, which you may use when we are alone. Later, you too will be given a new name."

"I have a perfectly good name, which was given to me at my baptism," hissed Emily, unmindful of the warning to keep her voice down.

Udepuri-Simone glanced quickly over her shoulder. "It is all right – no one has heard us," she said. "But speak quietly, all the same. We are all given new names here. Mine means 'Joyful One' and truly, I have not been unhappy since I was brought here."

"Against your will – you too?" said Emily.

She shrugged her shoulders. "I was not first asked for my permission, if that is what you mean. But how am I worse off? I was maid to a British lady in Poona, a haughty, pretentious woman, who was impatient with me because I could not learn her impossible language.

How I detested her! One night, I was walking in the woods alone . . ." she lowered her eyes for a second, laughing softly. "To be truthful, I had been meeting a young footman and was returning home. Then, suddenly, riders came up behind me, I was snatched into the saddle and brought here, after a journey of several days. *Romanesque*, is it not? but alas, the conclusion was not so, not for me, for they had made a mistake, those horsemen. It was you they wanted, not me."

"Me? How could that be, when I was shipwrecked only days ago? Besides, I am no one to kidnap at such great pains, only the daughter of an official of the East India Company."

"You yourself might be insignificant, but you are English, and that is what they wanted. They believed I was English, and there was consternation when on my arrival here I was discovered not to be so. Still, I was allowed to remain – indeed, obliged to do so – and treated well, so now I live a life of some luxury, instead of running about all day at the beck and call of that odious memsahib."

"Simone, why is it they want an English girl, and have gone to all this trouble to procure one?" Emily asked.

"Why, it is for His Highness' only son, Prince Dara," she explained. "He returned only last year from the English University, since when he has been bored and restless, and satisfied by none of the usual distractions. Talk in the mahal is that nothing will please him but to have an English concubine and companion, to remind him of his time in England, and to converse with him in the language of that country. Alas for me, that I did not try harder to learn English," she lamented, "for I have seen Prince Dara in the courtyard, and he is *un jeune homme très magnifique!*"

Emily shuddered with revulsion.

"But this is outrageous! I am a subject of Queen Victoria, and I will not be the concubine of some spoiled prince!" she declared.

"You are a subject of Prince Murad now, like every one of us here, and since Prince Dara is his heir, his sun and moon, it will be sensible, indeed realistic of you, to please him in any way you can," Simone reminded her soberly.

"I have no intention of remaining here and being treated in this manner," Emily rejoined spiritedly. "If they will not voluntarily let me go, I must somehow find a way to escape."

"*Chérie*, be reasonable," Simone pleaded. "Do not make life more difficult for yourself. Existence here will be more than pleasant for you, should you find favour in the eyes of Prince Dara. You will lack nothing. Clothes, jewels, servants, your own sumptuous rooms – nothing will be denied you."

"Only my freedom," she pointed out.

"Freedom to do what? To return to England and live in your cold climate, to marry some ordinary young man who can give you not one hundredth of the luxuries you will enjoy here? *Zut!*" Simone spat contemptuously. "You are a fool, *Emilie*."

Her expression softened. "Ah – I know. You have been gently reared, you have no experience, is it? There is nothing, I promise you, to be afraid of in the love of a man."

Emily flushed, for indeed, she was ignorant of men, and no one had ever spoken to her thus of physical love. Her mother had told her the barest facts of life, that she would be married one day, must submit herself to her husband, and that children would be born to her. Once she had said with bitterness that love would betray her, that through it she would know only suffering, but Emily did not, could not, know what she meant. Her only knowledge of love was through the romance of poetry and literature, which she had so copiously read.

"Besides," went on Simone, "to escape from here is impossible. Within the harem, its apartments and gardens, we move freely, but the whole is walled and guarded most carefully. Not an inner door without a huge, muscular female guard, not an outer gate without an armed eunuch, not a thing comes into or goes out of the harem without the closest inspection. To attempt to escape would be madness, and furthermore, a waste of time. Do not even dream of it. Accept what fate has given you, and make the best of it."

Emily said no more on the subject, but determined in her own mind to make the attempt. It had to be possible, she could not remain here as the plaything of some Eastern prince, until he should tire of her.

"I must now inform Qadir Bibi Bano that you are awake," said Simone, "or soon she will be here to find out for herself, and I shall be in trouble again."

"Who is she, and why does she wield so much authority over you?" Emily asked.

Simone lowered her voice even further. "I told you, within the harem, her word is law. She rules the women's quarters. She is fair and just, but firm, and almost impossible to fool. It is she who notes our talents and virtues, and how they may be used, also our faults and peccadilloes. All is reported to higher authority, and you may be sure, she has eyes and ears everywhere."

Rather like the headmistress of one of the select academies for young ladies to which her father had wanted to send her, Emily imagined grimly, although she had never attended one, and was sure this was far from what he'd had in mind. She was all the more determined to escape. She would stifle here, in this atmosphere of confined luxury.

For the rest of that day, she was never alone for a moment. Under the supervision of Qadir Bibi Bano, she was bathed in a sunken bath, deliciously scented, and then her body was expertly massaged and rubbed with perfumed oil. Her hair, too, was washed and brushed, rubbed and dressed, until it shone with a bronze lustre darker than its usual shade. At each step in the process, Qadir Bibi Bano inspected and indicated her approval, and Emily winced at the inspection, since no one but her mother and her personal maid had ever seen her naked.

Innumerable saris of brilliant, delicate silk were produced and tried on, and a selection chosen for her use. She stood mute and unsmiling as the silken folds were wrapped round her; it was better thus to maintain her dignity, rather than to give way to screaming and useless resistance. Silently, inwardly, the whole of the time, she repeated the words, I will *not* stay, I *will* not stay, forcing herself to believe them.

She ate nothing but a little fruit and a cup of buttermilk which was delicious, waving away all the spiced dishes which were brought for her. She could not eat. But she could look, and this she did, as she was led from one part of the *zenana* to another, for it was like nothing she had ever seen before.

Each *mahal*, or palace, interconnected with the rest, melting into one another, maze-like, by means of endless corridors and doors and halls. She glimpsed fabulous rooms with gloriously patterned Persian carpets on the floors, beautiful tapestries on the walls, divans and couches covered with embroidered silk and strewn with brocade cushions. Marble pillars were garlanded with fresh flowers, and looking upwards gave no relief from the continuing impact of such beauty, since the ceilings were inlaid with silver and precious stones.

Yet for all this glory of stone and fabric and gem, the loveliness of these quarters depended heavily on something infinitely more simple. Water – burbling in narrow channels set in the marble floors, reflecting each scene in pools alive with goldfish, and everywhere, fountains everlastingly splashing.

The harem opened out into seductive gardens of roses and jasmine, there were tree-shaded walks, alleys, shady grottoes, paths and streams.

Speechless with amazement at all this splendour, the like of which she had never even imagined could exist, Emily was, if possible, even more determined to escape. But all she had seen only confirmed what Simone had already told her. High walls surrounded the gardens. Strongly-built female guards were in evidence throughout the interior, armed guards were posted at all the exterior gates. Huge black sentinels, with skins which shone like coal, padded the corridors, silently.

"Who are those men?" Emily whispered to Simone. The French girl shook her head. "Not men – eunuchs," she replied. "*Castrati* – you understand? They are Nubians, shipped across from Africa by Arab traders and smuggled into Bilkhondar behind the backs of the British, through their territory. Do not underestimate them, *chérie*. They are incredibly strong and agile, and their experiences have made them evil. They would strangle you, given half a chance."

Emily shivered. This was nothing but a prison, a gilded, cloying, beautiful prison, and beneath the ostentatious luxury, menace stalked these warm, sensuous quarters. She could *not* remain here.

And she . . . what was she, what had they made of her? Catching sight of her reflection in one of the pools, she gasped, for there was little left of Miss Emily Hunter in this painted courtesan in her emerald sari, her skin and hair gleaming, her eyebrows plucked and arched, her fingertips encarmined, her neck hung with ropes of pearls, her fingers sparkling with rings, her slender waist encircled by a golden belt. She had been all but extinguished, and in that moment, it was a wonder that she did not break down and weep.

But she did not. She held tightly to that inner self she knew was still alive, and waited for night, when she was finally and blessedly alone on her couch in the alcove.

When all was quiet, and even the chased silver hanging lamps no longer burned, only red and blue bowls with burning wicks casting flickering shadows on the walls, she slipped soundlessly from her bed and stole along the corridor. Creeping quietly from mahal to mahal, past closed apartment doors, past sleeping figures in alcoves, picking her way towards what? She did not know, directed only by her blind desire to escape.

Miraculously, she saw only one female guard, and her she dodged by gliding quickly behind a marble pillar. In front of her, at the end of a long, dimly-lit corridor, she saw an enormous, brass-studded door, with no guards in front of it. Her good fortune was unbelievable, the guards were sleeping, or they were idling their time away somewhere. She must hurry, hurry, before they came back. She began to run towards the door, her slippered feet gathering speed on the cool marble. . . . Just as she had almost reached it, two huge eunuchs, armed with spears, sprang out of the shadows and barred her way, their faces impassive.

Emily gasped and spun round, away from them, and at once came face to face with a semicircle of female sentinels. She had not seen them in her cautious progress along the corridors, but from hidden corners they had observed her, and all the way she had been silently followed. Simone was right. The mahals never truly slept, and there was no possibility of escaping. She sank to the floor, her head buried in her hands, beyond tears, beyond fear, conscious only of a leaden despair.

She was lifted up and carried back to her bed, under the supervision of the ever-watchful Qadir Bibi Bano, and there she lay, with two of the grim-faced female sentries standing guard, one at the head, one at the foot of her divan, for the remainder of the night. A few feet away down the corridor, still in full view of her, one of the fierce black eunuchs stood with arms folded, watching her, like some huge cat, waiting to spring if she so much as moved.

It no longer mattered to Emily that they were there. She turned her back on them in a gesture of rejection, and lay curled on her divan, silent and virtually immobile. She had no more tears left with which to express her fear and frustration and distress in this alien place, which she seemed doomed never to leave. In the end, exhaustion claimed her and she fell into a deep sleep.

CHAPTER
THREE

In the morning, it was Simone who woke her, gently shaking her shoulder.

"Come, *Emilie*. You have been permitted to sleep late, but now there is much to be done if you are to appear beautiful once more."

Emily saw that the guards were gone, and Simone was attended only by two smiling young women, less finely dressed and more servile than those Emily had previously seen.

"These will be your personal slaves from now on," Simone said. "Their names are Gulal and Yasmin."

"Slaves – why should I require slaves?" Emily asked derisively. "I am quite capable of looking after myself."

"What nonsense! In England, did you not have a lady's maid? *Bien sûr*, you did. Here it is a little different, you have slaves. They are harmless creatures. Now see, they are downcast because you don't want them."

Emily smiled kindly at the two slave-girls. "Oh, it's not their fault," she said, adding unrepentantly, "They are a distinct improvement on last night's watchdogs!"

"Hush!" said Simone. "Mind your tongue, and be advised by me. Qadir Bibi Bano is wise, more than you could understand. She knows you will now have real-ised that what you tried to do last night is impossible, and will never attempt it again." Her voice dropped even further. "Indiscreet behaviour, *chérie*, is punish-able by death, so tread carefully along these halls. One thing alone saved you last night. You were chosen and brought here by the agents of Prince Murad, for his son, Prince Dara, who has yet has not seen you."

"You mean to tell me I could have been put to death, simply for trying to get out of here?" Emily gasped.

"Lives have been snuffed out like candles for less than that," Simone remarked soberly. "This is not England. While you are awaiting Prince Dara's approval, no one will harm a hair of your head. But you are alone here, Emily. You need his approval, and his protection – desperately. Your fate depends on him."

A shudder of revulsion shook Emily's slim body. In order to survive in this monstrous world, where a woman's life apparently meant very little, she had to allow herself to be used by this pampered princeling.

"Oh, that's horrible! I can't," she said wretchedly. "Perhaps he will find me ugly, perhaps he won't like me at all and will send me away."

Simone looked at her appraisingly. "I do not think any man would find you ugly, Emily, even with dark rings round your eyes from insufficient sleep, and your hair all in a tangle. But I beg you, do not hope for this. You will never be allowed to leave here. If His Highness does not care for you, you will be cast aside and used as a slave, or given to one of the lesser nobles for his harem. Prince Dara is your best hope, so we must do what we can."

So it all began again, the bathing and massaging, the painting and embellishing, the degradation of her body, in order that it might be still further degraded. Emily felt as if she were being prepared for sacrifice, a victim in some pagan rite, and she was powerless to do anything but submit to it.

Finally, dressed in a sari of palest orange, bejewelled and perfumed, she was conducted by Qadir

Bibi Bano, followed at a respectful distance by Simone and the slave girls, and the envious glances of the other inmates of the harem, along the corridors, not knowing where she was being taken, aware that there was nothing for her but to meet whatever was in store for her, to summon up her courage and hope it would see her through.

Nonetheless, she gasped in astonishment when she was ushered into a suite of rooms, the elegance and luxury of which surpassed anything she had yet seen.

"These are your quarters henceforth," said Simone, unable to keep her envy from filtering through her translation.

"For me?" Emily said, taking a few steps inside. Qadir Bibi Bano smiled and spread out her hand in an expansive gesture, inviting her to explore, and the girl could not resist doing so. Her eyes took in the soft Persian carpet, exquisitely patterned with birds and flowers in soft blues, golds and reds, the gorgeous tapestries on the walls depicting elegant Mogul lords enjoying the hunt, while their ladies displayed their brightly-hued robes and slender limbs, and fine Persian profiles. There were couches spread with brocade coverlets, and in the bedchamber, silken hangings draped around an enormous divan, clearly not meant for one. Emily fingered the fine, almost transparent silk with distaste, and moved on to inspect the sunken bathroom, with its beautiful marble floors and walls, an astounding azure blue.

The apartment opened on to a breathtakingly lovely garden, walled and private. Roses climbed the walls, filling the air with their perfume, and in the centre two white marble fountains splashed in unison.

"For you," Simone confirmed, and in low tones added, "Did I not tell you so?"

Emily could find no solace in all this magnificence. She did not require it. It did not accord her any more freedom. True, she had privacy in that there was a door she could close on the rest of the harem, so that she might be alone and unobserved, but she had noted immediately that the door had locks on the outside only. She could not barricade herself inside and refuse admittance. All she had here was an illusion of sanctuary. The rooms, and not only the rooms but she herself, could be invaded at any time, with or without her permission.

"The slave-girls will be outside, and should you require anything, you have only to call," Simone said.

"And you? Where will you be?" Emily asked in sudden panic, reluctant to lose the only friend she felt she had.

"Back there, with the less fortunate ones," she answered with a grimace. *"Au revoir, Emilie, et belle chance."*

Evening was approaching, the swift dusk had already enveloped the garden. The girl named Gulal lit the silver lamps which spangled ornate, ever-shifting patterns on the walls and ceilings. Then all of them withdrew, leaving Emily alone in her new domains, alone and uncertain. She longed for something to do, to distract her mind from her fears, but there was nothing. For all the magnificence of the rooms, there was not a book of any description to be found, nor a sheet of paper and pen, nor a musical instrument. Was a woman required only to be beautiful and agreeable? she wondered.

She walked abstractedly back and forth in a state of intense agitation. She could go no further than the walls of her garden and her apartment had only the one exit leading back into the main halls of the harem. There was nowhere to run, nowhere to hide, no way of escaping the unpleasant fate in store for her.

Except one. There was always one option open to her, she thought if she chose to take it. She could take her own life. She could demand water for the vast, sunken bath, and drown herself in it, or she could unwind the silken hangings from the bed and hang herself. If she acted quickly and decisively, and really meant to do it, no one could prevent her. She could cheat them all, including the odious Prince Dara, who thought she was his for the taking.

She stood arrested in her pacing, mulling over this new and surprising thought that had occurred to her. She thought; my parents are dead, I am alone and unlikely ever to return to the world I know. I am facing imminent disgrace, and at best, a short spell as the plaything of this lascivious monster of a man who has innocent European girls abducted to satisfy his appetites. What reason is there for me to go on living?

Emily sighed deeply. She considered the possibility of suicide, openly and truthfully, and she rejected it, not, she felt, because she feared death very much at this moment, or because she lacked the resolution to do it. But there was this small, truant flame inside her, which still, in spite of everything, desired life. To die at eighteen, with one's youth and beauty unspent, and half one's life untasted, was not for her. She had survived a shipwreck, the tragic death of her father, survived that dreadful journey to Bilkhondar. And I shall survive *this*, she told herself defiantly.

Then there were footsteps, many footsteps in the outer corridor, there was a flurry of shouted commands, and all of this centred on the door to her room. She stood as still as a statue, hands clenched at her sides, gazing at the door as if mesmerised. Her heart was hammering loudly, she could feel herself shaking, and all her bravado melted away.

The door was flung open, and two guards entered, armed with deadly curved scimitars. They stood a few paces inside the room, one at either side of the doorway, and a man entered and stood between them. He stood there, saying nothing, simply looking her slowly up and down, seeing a slender girl who was clearly English, despite her pale orange sari, a peach-skinned girl whose hair, oiled and dressed in an elaborate and formal chignon, was still the colour of spun gold and sunlight. She was very young, and although she held herself proudly erect, obviously very frightened.

As for Emily, she could not tear her fascinated gaze from him, for she was looking at the most superbly handsome young man she had ever seen. Tall, slim, and yet well made, he had a skin of palest olive, his features were as finely cut as those of the Mogul lords on her tapestries, and his brilliant dark eyes were almond-shaped, as were theirs. It was an arresting face, redeemed from too much perfection by just a hint of sensuality and laughter about the mouth – visible, although at the moment, he was grave and unsmiling. And this perfection was repeated in everything he was wearing, the gold-embroidered cream silk tunic, the trousers sashed with a cummerbund of cloth of gold, and tucked into soft leather boots.

At length, she came to her senses and dropped her gaze. And because this was so obviously a royal personage, she sank, as gracefully as she could, into the low obeisance she had practised so many times at home, book on head, to improve her deportment.

"Oh, please," he said, in perfectly pronounced English she could have heard any day in her mother's drawing-room. "Let us have no more of that." Extending a slim hand, a-glitter with rings, he lifted her to her feet.

Emily did not know precisely what she had expected to find in His Royal Highness, Prince Dara, heir to the throne of Bilkhondar, but her mind had conjured up the image of a spoiled, gilded, arrogant young man who was also a monster of depravity. She knew that his father's power over his subjects was absolute, and that he, too, had a measure of authority beyond anything she had met. She had seen, too, that this court was conducted as if it were living in the seventeenth century instead of the latter part of the nineteenth, and that here there were no restraints on cruelty and license, for those who wielded power.

Furthermore, this was an harem, and she understood well enough the purpose for which women were kept here. Although she was entirely innocent, and her imagination had resolutely refused to dwell on details when visualising their first encounter, she knew she was expecting something to happen to her which should not happen to any well-brought-up girl of her class until her wedding night, and she had steeled herself inwardly to deal with emotions such as shame and fear, possibly even with pain and revulsion.

Prince Dara motioned to one of the guards to close the door behind him, but he did not dismiss them, and they stood there, scimitars at the ready, almost as if, she thought crazily, they expected *her* to attack their master.

She was not reassured by the fact that he spoke her language as well as she did, or because his demeanour, whilst proud and dignified, could not be described as arrogant. He was still the man responsible for bringing her here and keeping her here, forcibly, against her will. So when he advanced a few steps towards her and lifted her out of her curtsey, she shrank instinctively from his touch, putting several feet of space between them.

"Please be seated," he said, calmly and courteously, just as if he and she had met at a soirée in England. He indicated one of the couches and Emily obeyed, never taking her eyes from him as she passed, for who knew when he might choose to spring at her?

But the Prince merely waited until she was seated, before sitting down himself on another couch, a respectable distance from her.

"I extend my sympathy to you over the death of your father," he said. "I trust you are well now, and recovered from the after-effects of the shipwreck."

Emily swallowed hard. The last thing she wanted was to antagonise him, but a stubborn pride in her wanted him to realise that she was not a willing prisoner here.

"As well as is possible, under the circumstances," she replied coolly, clasping her hands together to stop them from shaking.

He disregarded this, treating it with princely unconcern.

"I hear that you have not been eating too well," he said. Clearly, everything about her had been accurately and minutely reported to him. "That is understandable. You have not been well, and our food is no doubt strange to you. But it is essential, now, for the sake of your health, that you take some food. I have ordered some kedgeree. Perhaps you will eat a little. It is only rice and fish."

He clapped his hands, and slaves brought in the food on a silver dish. This was familiar fare to Emily, it had been served at home whenever her father was there on leave. And this, prepared in the palace kitchens, smelled delicious. Her appetite, always good in the past, began to revive, or perhaps it was a reaction of relief because this very personable man had, so far, treated her with politeness. She found herself eating hungrily, and enjoying it.

"Good, good," he said approvingly. "That is much better," and fruit and wine were brought. The wine was served in chased silver goblets, and the Prince drank some, too. When she could eat and drink no more, he had the dishes taken away.

"Now, tell me," he said, "do you find the apartment comfortable? Is there anything further you require?"

The food had restored Emily's spirit, and she forgot her caution sufficiently to venture, "Your Highness must know that the rooms are beyond criticism. I shall be very comfortable . . . if I must be here."

The dark eyes held an unfathomable glint, as he replied, "I am afraid that you must."

He rose to his feet, and Emily stiffened; she saw a faint smile touch his lips as he noted this involuntary movement.

"I will leave you now," he said. "Goodnight. I trust you will sleep well."

His departure was as brisk as his arrival, and in his wake followed the guards, who had stood immobile by the door the whole of the time.

Emily stood up, pressed the palms of her hands to her temples, and let out a sigh of relieved tension. Prince Dara's visit, for which she had been so keyed up with fear and anticipation, was over, and she did not begin to understand. He had been cool, polite and considerate, he had not touched her, nor had he displayed the slightest interest in her as a woman. And yet everything she had been told in the harem led her to believe that his intentions towards her were carnal. She was deeply bewildered, and in her heart of hearts, she confessed to herself, still afraid.

There was a light tap on the door, and Simone's voice called out, "It is only me – may I come in?"

Without waiting for a reply, the French girl slipped into the room, her eyes sparkling.

"I have come myself to prepare you for bed, instead of sending the slave-girls," she said. "I could not wait to hear about the Prince's visit. They are talking of little else in the zenana, you are the envy of everyone. Is he not handsome? Not one girl but would wish to be in your shoes tonight, myself included!"

Simone took the pins from Emily's hair, and began to brush it with long, sweeping strokes. But her eager curiosity was too much for her to contain, and she paused, brush in midair.

"His visit was not overlong, and he did not dismiss the guards, but still, stranger things have happened here. You must have pleased His Highness, since you are still here in these rooms, enjoying privileged treatment."

Emily sat still, at a loss how to answer. For one thing, she had not been brought up to discuss so frankly the intimate details of her life, even had there been any to discuss. And she was reluctant to admit to Simone that most of the time that the prince had been in her quarters, she had spent eating. If she were envied, it was because everyone believed she was Prince Dara's new concubine; this supposed relationship was her only source of respect inside these walls. Should it be known that her position so far was spurious, she lost her only advantage. She would be the object of ridicule, and rumour would spread like wildfire to the effect that she had *not* pleased His Highness.

Perhaps, she thought, with a flash of mortification.

she had not, and she wondered why she should care, unless it were a streak of perverse feminine pride which would not let her believe she had been found undesirable.

She drew herself up, and turned to face Simone, ready to brazen this issue out.

"Simone, you are my only friend, and I shall be glad of your companionship," she said, "but what happens in this room, between Prince Dara and myself, is not for the edification of the harem in general, and I should prefer not to discuss it."

"*Tiens!*" said the French girl, amused but unmoved. "You learn very quickly to play the great lady."

She put down the brush and walked quickly to the bedchamber, where she stood for a moment surveying the chaste, undisturbed bed. "So that's how it is!" she said, flinging back the silken coverlet.

"What are you doing?" Emily asked in a small voice.

"I am helping you," said Simone. "Nothing has happened in here tonight, that is plain enough to me. You cannot fool me so easily, Emily, but together we may be able to convince the rest of the harem."

Emily's feigned haughtiness collapsed. "I don't understand," she said.

"Of course you don't, you poor, innocent child," Simone said, more kindly. "If the slave-girls had come here just now, they would have reported at once to Qadir Bibi Bano that neither you nor the bed appear to have been touched. And did your mother never tell you that you would most likely bleed on your wedding night?"

Emily shook her head. "I was never close enough to marriage to require telling anything about it, and for the past year, my poor mother was too ill to think about such things."

Simone made a great performance of ruffling up the bed, and stood back, pleased with her handiwork.

"Ah well, never mind. Qadir Bibi Bano, knowing nothing of the way a girl of your social standing is reared in England, will assume that you were not a virgin before tonight."

"But I was – I mean, I *am*," Emily said indignantly.

"I know that, and so do you, but no one else need know," Simone said patiently.

"The guards know we never retired to the bed-chamber. They were here the whole time."

"They are not harem guards, but Prince Dara's personal bodyguards. They would die rather than divulge his private affairs, and might well die if they did," Simone said darkly. "Come, let us get you out of that sari, you look too immaculate for your own good."

Clad in a loose robe, with her hair around her shoulders, Emily said, puzzled, "Simone – about Prince Dara. . . ."

"Ah, Emily!" Simone smiled. "Did you expect the Prince to pounce upon you and ravish you on the spot? He is not a street-corner rapist, but a cultured, educated man, in every sense. Most probably he, too, recognises a frightened virgin when he sees one. He has only to lift a finger and any of those women out there would be his – willingly. Perhaps he would prefer you to come to him that way."

"Then he will have a long time to wait, for I never shall!" Emily declared.

"Do not try his patience too far. Remember he is a prince, and accustomed to having his wishes obeyed unquestioningly," Simone warned her. "This little charade of ours will do for tonight, but not for long, *Emilie!*"

Despite the crowded events of the evening, or

perhaps because of them, Emily slept well in her new quarters, and in the morning, the slave-girl Yasmin smilingly brought her food and prepared her bath. Apart from the inevitable beautification session, she was left more or less to herself, asked no questions, required to do nothing. To be alone was a luxury to her after the constant attentions of the last few days, and she revelled in her privacy. Prince Dara had visited her, and by his visit conferred his seal of approval on her. He must have given orders that she was to remain in her luxurious quarters and be treated with every considera-tion, and so it was. But Emily remembered what Simone had said, and as evening approached, she was on edge, anticipating his next visit. What if last night had been merely a reprieve? She did not think she could bear to live this way, in constant suspense and uncer-tainty.

She tensed as once again she heard the hard, male footsteps approaching along the corridor. But it was not Prince Dara, only a great retinue of servants, carrying what looked like . . . yes, bookshelves! And armful upon armful of books. Emily gasped as the books were stacked in piles on the floor of her apartment; she waited only until the door had closed behind the last of the servants and then she was across the room, eager to get her hands among all this bounty.

And these were not only books – they were English books, many of which she had in the library of her home at Overhampton, books she would have chosen herself, had the opportunity been hers. It was like a dream fulfilled, almost too good to be true, and Emily was down on her knees on the floor among volumes of Keats and Shelley, turning the pages eagerly, almost crying with delight at these dear, lost friends who had been restored to her.

So absorbed was she in her reading that when the Prince did come, she was unaware of his arrival until the moment the door opened, and he stood there looking at her, once again with his guards at either side of him.

"Do not disturb yourself," he said, as she made to scramble to her feet. He smiled, and the handsome face was irradiated. She thought, unwillingly, that if they had met under normal circumstances, and he had smiled at her like that, it would have been impossible not to like him, not to think that here was a man who possessed considerable charm, presence and personality. But here, in the harem, she knew that there was another side to him that was altogether less pleasant, otherwise she would not be here.

He motioned to the guards, and they sheathed their swords and adopted a more relaxed stance, whilst still remaining by the door.

"I see you love books, Miss Hunter," he said, and Emily could not hide the pleasure she felt, it was written on her face.

"Oh yes, and what a selection you have! Only, they are all mixed up. I don't know where to begin," she said breathlessly.

"Here, let me help you," he offered, and joined her, kneeling on the carpet amongst the piles of books. "Do you enjoy novels?" – picking up a volume – "Here is Mrs. Gaskell's *North and South*. And Charles Dickens, a fine writer."

"Wonderful!" Emily agreed. "I love poetry, too. Oh, look! Here is a volume of Lord Byron's verse. How splendid!"

Time sped by as they happily arranged the various works of poetry and literature in suitable juxtaposition on the shelves, and Emily almost forgot that she was in the harem of a tyrannical despot, and that this man beside her, busily examining the titles on the tooled leather bindings, was his son, to satisfy whose whim she had been abducted and incarcerated here.

Finally, Prince Dara sat back on his heels, surveying the results of their labour.

"These are more than books to me," he said pensively. "They are memories of a life I lived, which is gone. They are afternoons on the playing-fields, long hours undisturbed in the college library. They are the chimes of bells on Oxford's many churches, the slow English dusk, the boats on the river. The friends with whom I used to talk for hours. Perhaps that is what I miss most – friendship, the companionship of people who did not need to impress me or win my favour."

While he was speaking so nostalgically of England, Emily was aware of a strange, unbidden sympathy springing up in her heart. And then she reminded herself that he, who had loved her country, and missed so many things about it, could still condemn her to permanent separation from her home and her own people, and her heart became hardened again.

"It is clear that Your Highness realises that there are some things one cannot command, with all the money and power in the world," she said acidly. "Friendship is one of them."

He looked up, saw the fear and hostility that the blue eyes were unable to conceal, and the brief rapport between them was gone.

He frowned.

"I know full well the limitations of my position, Miss Hunter, without your having to draw my attention to them," he said, his voice quiet, dignified, but with a hint of warning in it. "Do not presume to lecture me. It would be ill advised of you."

"I would not so presume, Your Highness," Emily said, with heavy irony. "I, too, know the limitations of my position."

They held each other's gaze for a full half-minute, every second of which was measured by the beat of Emily's heart. She was a battleground where pride fought fear, where resentment and natural caution strove to get the upper hand, and she was never more conscious of this man's power than she was at that moment, half expecting him to strike her to the ground, or to call the guards and have her dragged off to some unspeakable fate.

He did neither. To her utter discomfiture, Prince Dara actually laughed, in genuine appreciation of her riposte. Then, leaving her still sitting there on the floor, he got up and paced across the room.

"Tell me, Miss Hunter," he said, polite and formal once more, "do you play the pianoforte?"

Emily struggled to her feet, smoothing down the folds of her still unaccustomed sari.

"Naturally," she said, with dignity. "My education was not neglected, and my mother believed it to be a necessary accomplishment for a lady to play and sing a little."

"Good. Excellent," said Prince Dara, and with that he left her.

The pianoforte arrived early the following day, much to the amazement of the rest of the harem, who had never before seen so strange an instrument. With it came an unsigned note, delivered on a small silver tray.

"Money may not buy friendship, but it can conjure up pianofortes, even in Bilkhondar," read the elegant script. It did indeed appear that Prince Dara had only to say the word and his wish was granted, she thought ruefully.

Seating herself on the piano stool, she riffled through the stack of sheet music he had sent with the instrument, and soon, sounding oddly out of place in these exotic surroundings, the strains of a Mozart minuet, followed by "Believe me if all those endearing young charms", drifted out on the scented air.

"To be quite honest with you, I did not conjure up the pianoforte out of thin air," he said lightly, the same evening. "I had it shipped out from England some months ago, but I must admit, I have never really mastered it. No matter – now you can play for me."

Emily felt anger and frustration rise in her throat. Books for her to read, a pianoforte for her to play, fabulous silks and jewels for her to wear, all at his discretion, at his command, as if she were some kind of exotic animal to be kept in a cage to amuse him. But she was not, she was plain Emily Hunter from Overhampton, she was a living human being with real emotions.

She crashed both hands down on the keys, in a loud, discordant jangle of noise.

"I will not!" she said, her young face clear and firm, with only the slightest tremor of apprehension. She saw the guards at the door place their hands on the hilts of their swords. Prince Dara leaned one elbow on the shining black surface of the pianoforte, and regarded her steadily, chin resting on his hand.

"Play," he said softly, but commandingly.

"No!" said Emily. "No, I will not. And you can do what you like, but you cannot make me. Kill me if you want to, I don't care! I hate you!"

She jumped to her feet, poised as if for flight, but his lean, strong fingers closed around her wrist and held her captive. "Let me go!"

"Not until you have explained yourself," he said

calmly. "I want to know just what it is you think I am going to do to you. Why should I kill you? I only want you to play the pianoforte. Surely you do not play as badly as that?"

"It is easy for you to jest," she cried bitterly. "There is very little humour in this situation for me, held prisoner here, forbidden to leave, separated from my countrymen and the only life I have ever known."

She saw the stern lines of his face relax, and he shook his head, groaning a little.

"Is that the kind of man you think I am?" he demanded. "You think it was on my orders you were brought here?"

He let go quite abruptly, but she remained standing where she was; her impulse to run was gone.

"What else am I to think?" she whispered.

He sighed deeply. "Indeed, what else should you believe?" he said wearily. "Sit down, please . . . Emily."

It was because of this, that for the first time he addressed her by her Christian name, that she sank obediently on to the piano stool, looking up enquiringly at him.

"But they told me I was brought here at your request," she said.

"No," he stated firmly, "that is not so. I would not have ordered the kidnapping of a young English lady. I have lived in your country, and I know that women are brought up and treated quite differently there. I understand, believe me, exactly the kind of shock this court must have given you. There are times when, although I was born and raised here, I feel adrift, unsure of where I truly belong."

He paused. "But my father – how shall I explain it? – still lives in the seventeenth century. To him, a woman is just a chattel, to be obtained and discarded at his pleasure. He was concerned because on my return, I could not settle down, I was restless and dissatisfied. He asked why I did not amuse myself in the harem, as princes traditionally do, and I suppose I am guilty up to a point, since I replied, somewhat facetiously, that I might if it contained an intelligent young English-speaking lady, with whom I might converse as I had been accustomed to doing in that country."

Emily could only listen, silent and spellbound, as he continued.

"I should have known my father would take me at my word. For him, to express a desire is to achieve satisfaction of it. First of all, we had the wretched business of the French girl who was kidnapped mistakenly, and I thought he would realise the futility of the notion. And then there was you."

Emily sat quietly, taking in all of this. She had wronged him by believing he had instigated her capture, but she was never more glad to find herself in the wrong. She could look at him now, and see the real man, not the image of the depraved Eastern potentate she had set up in his stead, before she had even met him.

"Then if you did not want me here," she said, "and I do not wish to remain, why am I still in Bilkhondar? Why may I not go home?"

He said, "Because it would not be possible. Even at my request, my father would never consent to your leaving. No one goes out from the harem, and particularly not you. There would be a diplomatic incident should it be discovered that a subject of Queen Victoria had been restrained in a prince's harem. It would give the British the chance my father fears they are always seeking, the excuse to repudiate their treaty promising

Bilkhondar autonomy, and to invade and incorporate us into their territory. They have the military capacity to do so."

Still Emily did not move. So it was true, there was no way out, and she would be here for the rest of her life. She was not the chosen one of Prince Dara, with all that that implied, nor was she any longer Emily Hunter of Overhampton, free to make her own future. She was here simply as the result of a stupid misunderstanding. No one wanted her, but they would not permit her to leave. Here she was, and here she had to stay. It was unfair, unfair!

"Emily," Prince Dara said, and his voice was surprisingly gentle, "will you play the pianoforte, now?"

She looked up at him, her eyes full of unshed tears.

"Your Highness, I will play," she said. And very haltingly, from memory, she began to play a Beethoven sonata. In some way she did not yet understand, the music fused together the disparate elements of the situation, the sadness of the beautiful room with the moonlight filtering in from the garden, her own despair, and his inability to help her, and afforded her a measure of consolation.

CHAPTER
FOUR

IN the morning, the birds were singing in her garden, the roses smelled sweet, the fountains splashed, and already the sun was warm.

Emily thought at once of the dramatic scene she had played out with Prince Dara, it was in her mind so vividly that she could almost feel the hard, relentless grip of his hand on her arm, almost hear her own voice sobbing out, "I hate you!" But equally real was her recollection of the gentleness in his eyes and his voice as he explained the sad farce which had led to her capture.

Did she hate him? Almost certainly not, she admitted to herself. She had been in terror of him to begin with, but even that had been largely fear of the idea her own mind had projected. It seemed ludicrous, in the light of her present knowledge of him, slight though that was, to imagine this proud, cultured, civilised man subjecting any woman to a crude and undesired assault. But it was also difficult to envisage him being held at arm's length by a woman if he really wanted her, and this led her to only one conclusion. His Royal Highness Prince Dara did not find her attractive enough to be worth the effort of seducing. To him, she was only a reminder of things he had found pleasant in England. He enjoyed conversing with her, they shared a deep interest in literature, and to a lesser extent, music, and he was probably being truthful when he said he felt the lack of any real friends in this rarefied and feudal place where his every whim was catered for.

She should have been relieved by this discovery, and in a way, she told herself, she was, but contrarily she found herself frowning into her hand mirror. For it did not take an expert to realise that Prince Dara had taste – it was evident in the clothes he wore, in his appreciation of literature, in a thousand little things about his manner and his person which declared him to be a man of fastidious habit and discrimination. It followed that this judgment also applied to his choice of women, and she, Emily, obviously did not meet his standards.

And no wonder, she said disgustedly to herself, remembering the painted effigy they had made of her, and would shortly do again if she permitted them to. It came to Emily, with a small thrill of pleasure, that she did not have to submit to all these ministrations if she did not wish to. So long as her orders did not contradict any expressly laid down by Prince Dara, her assumed position gave her enough power to exert her will against that of the Lady Protectress.

So she allowed the slave-girls to wash her hair and rub it with scented oils, and to massage her body, for now the initial barriers of shyness and inhibition were overcome, she had to admit that these attentions were pleasant and relaxing. But she refused absolutely to allow them to paint her nails or her face, or to dress her beautiful red-blonde hair in the elaborate styles they loved. She simply had it brushed and allowed it to hang loose to her shoulders.

"You cannot let His Highness see you like this, as if you have taken no trouble to prepare yourself," said Simone, deeply shocked. "He will be offended."

"He does not care one way or the other about how

I look," Emily said. "At least he will see me as I am."

Simone summoned Qadir Bibi Bano, who looked Emily up and down with a gaze which bespoke years of experience of matters of the harem. She gave a faint smile, and a shrug, and spoke quickly and decisively to Simone, before going back about her own business.

"What did she say?" Emily demanded, ready for a battle if necessary.

"She said if the Prince liked you that way, I was not to interfere," the French girl said grudgingly. "But you are playing a dangerous game, *chérie*, and this is not a kindergarten. That hair of yours is little short of immoral."

When the Prince came to her room that night, he stood arrested in the doorway by the sight of Emily, her clear, pale skin untouched by any artifice, her glorious hair rippling over her shoulders. She had the fresh young beauty of a spring morning, and if his eyes narrowed, his lips compressed a little, she could not know that it was because she had stopped his heart for a moment.

"I see you have dispensed with the beauty treatments of the harem girls," he said, somewhat sardonically, she thought.

"Not entirely," she said, wincing a little at his disapproval. "I simply thought it was time I started looking like Emily Hunter again."

"You surprise me," he said. "I have an idea that in England you would have had to submit to the curling papers, is it not so?"

She did not know quite how to answer this, for she knew in her heart that he was right. She would have caused a minor sensation even in Overhampton, looking as she did now.

"I have decided to become an eccentric," she said lightly. "It is a tendency of Englishwomen living abroad."

"So you would submit to the conventions of your own country, but not to those of Bilkhondar?" he countered swiftly. Seeing the light of argument in the blue eyes, he made a gesture of bored disdain. "Wear your hair how you will. It is of no great importance," he said witheringly.

Still smarting from his indifference, she said, "As Your Highness says, it is unimportant. But there is one thing that is. I should like to learn the language. I came out knowing only a little Hindi, which has proved useless."

He said, "It would. We are too far south here for it to be much spoken. The vernacular is Marathi, which you will find most of the servants speak."

"I am beginning to pick up a little of that," she said. "But some of the harem ladies speak something quite different, and so does Qadir Bibi Bano, sometimes."

He glanced at her with new respect. "You have a quick ear for languages," he told her. "The official court, and anyone with a pretence to education, speaks Persian. It was the language of the old Mogul Empire, and as I told you, we are two hundred years behind the times here. You wish to learn Persian?"

"Very much."

"Then I shall have a tutor sent to you, and you may learn to read and write it, too." His lips curled in amusement. "Please veil yourself in his presence. He is a learned old scholar of at least seventy, but it is more than his life is worth to gaze on the faces of ladies of the harem."

And so, from necessity, Emily threw herself into the life of the harem, and she found that although they were confined within the women's quarters, they could still look out on the world, and snatches of it could come to them.

Every morning, Prince Murad presented himself to his subjects on a palace balcony known as the *jharoka*. Here they could in theory, submit petitions to him. From behind the latticework windows of a long, marble gallery, the women could watch, and Emily caught her first distant glimpses of the absolute ruler of this principality, a tall, hawk-faced man clad in silk pantaloons and richly embroidered gold tunic, an immense diamond aigrette studding the gold turban on his head.

From here, too, they could watch *durbar*, which was the ritual homage of the *omrahs*, or nobles, to their prince, gorgeously dressed and seated on splendidly caparisoned horses.

Within the harem, too, they were not without entertainment. There were dancing girls, and music played on stringed instruments accompanied by drums, which was strange to the ear at first, because, as Dara explained to her, it was purely melodic, without the harmonic structure all western music possesses. There was feasting, with every kind of meat; kid, goat, fowls, pigeons, fish, dishes spicy and sweet, pears, apples, grapes, pistachios and almonds, all served on gold and silver trays. There were story-tellers who read to them from behind screens, and there was parcheesi, a kind of outdoor chess, played with human pawns on a chequered courtyard, which always resulted in much amusement.

She envied Prince Dara who, when not occupied with such affairs of state as his father allowed him to deal with, sometimes hunted with his falcon, or rode in the hills on his favourite horse, which he whimsically named Mr. Scrooge. She longed to go with him, to feel the fresh, open air beyond the walls of the palace, but he shook his head and said it was absolutely forbidden.

From the old scholar who taught her Persian, she heard many stories of the Mogul Empire. He told her about Babur, the descendant of Tamerlane, who had swept down from Central Asia and established a tentative kingdom in India, of his shrewd, statesmanlike grandson, Akbar the Great, who expanded and consolidated the Empire, of *his* son, Jahangir, who drugged himself with opium and allowed his clever, ambitious wife to rule in his name. And of Shah Jehan, who loved his wife Mumtaz Mahal so much that after her death he built her an immense white marble mausoleum, the Taj Mahal, the most beautiful tomb the world had ever known.

"He talks a great deal about them," Emily said to the Prince one day, "and they are fascinating, but what have they to do with Bilkhondar?"

"Quite a lot," he said. "I am descended from them." And he told her the strange legend of his ancestry.

In 1659, the great Mogul Empire was in chaos at the end of a savage war of succession fought between the four sons of Shah Jehan. The emperor himself, aged and in poor health, was the prisoner of the victor, Aurangzeb, obsessive, shrewd and religiously fanatical, bitter from years of being his father's least favoured son. The eldest son, Dara Shikoh, mystic and dreamer, who had sat at the feet of Hindu gurus and eschewed Muslim orthodoxy, was also a helpless captive, soon to be put to death at his brothers orders.

The island fortress of Bhakkar, in the River Indus south of Multan, held in Dara Shikoh's name by the eunuch, Basant, had finally surrendered to Aurangzeb's troops, after a long, determined siege, and along with the fortress were surrendered several of Prince

Dara's infant grandchildren, who had been left there for safe-keeping. They were never heard of again, presumably murdered by Aurangzeb.

"But they did not all die," the present Prince Dara told her. "One, a small prince, was smuggled away by a faithful retainer, and brought, eventually, to Bilkhondar. When he came of age, he was married to the daughter of the ruler. Thus it is that we follow, even now, many of the customs of the Mogul Empire, long after it has ceased to exist in all but name anywhere else in India, and thus it is that I have the blood of the Great Moguls, of Akbar and Tamerlane, in my veins. Much good may it do me," he added drily.

"What do you mean?" she asked curiously. "Aren't you proud of this inheritance?"

"Proud? Yes, but Bilkhondar must look to its future, must move into the world of today. These are not words for everyone's ears," he told her solemnly. "My father would consider them dangerous, treasonable even. He sees himself as the heir of the Moguls, the guardian of their tradition, and will change nothing in this land. While he lives, I can do nothing, but I am his only legitimate son. My mother died when I was young, and he has shown no interest in taking another wife, but even if he does, and other children are born, I must some day inherit the throne."

Emily caught her breath.

"And then – when you do?"

"And then I shall pull Bilkhondar into this century. It will be hard. There will be powerful forces opposing me, religious leaders, omrahs with a vested interest in keeping things as they are, but I shall hold the balance of power, and I shall do it. It is necessary, Emily. Outside the luxury of this court, people live in degradation such as you have never seen, although there is plenty of poverty in England. We must have roads, schools, hospitals, we must have commerce and industry. And I fear we must have the British to help us achieve all this, in the beginning, although I should be called a traitor for saying it."

"Are you saying that you would hand over Bilkhondar to the British in return for this kind of help?" Emily asked carefully.

He sighed. "Not necessarily. I am merely thinking aloud, and without reaching any firm conclusions. But I suppose if there is no other way, then that is what I shall have to do. Why? Do you consider it heinous of me, to talk of giving up my birthright?"

"No," she said steadily, "not if it is in order to help your people. But it will not be easy to accomplish this and still maintain your involvement with the country, which I imagine you would wish to do."

He smiled ruefully. "I never said I expected it to be easy. But I dream of a different future for the Indian subcontinent, not just for Bilkhondar. I envision a day when they will be one, all the dominions Akbar ruled, and those he never conquered, when they will be ruled neither by princes nor foreign masters."

"Without the British?" Emily asked. It seemed a difficult idea to grasp, and he laughed. "You think your countrymen are here for ever? That India is theirs to rule in perpetuity? I don't believe so. They will go, eventually, but not yet. We have to have them first, use them, learn from them, and suffer through them. This is their time to rule, but one day they will be an anachronism. So will such as I," he added lightly. "The people will govern themselves one day, and then they will have no use for princes."

Listening to him talking to her in this way, she understood that this young man had come back from the West with ideas in his head which were considered daring and unorthodox even there. Here, as he himself admitted, they were too subversive to express, even for the treasured only son and heir of Prince Murad. That he had discussed these ideas with her was a declaration of trust, for here, where there were eyes and ears everywhere, it needed only the slightest indiscretion on her part, the merest casual, thoughtless comment to anyone in the harem, for Prince Murad to know what dangerous thoughts were in hs son's head. Emily shuddered, glad that they were sitting in the garden at the time, and the two guards, although in full view of them, were well out of earshot.

"I don't think you should speak of such things," she said, suddenly afraid for him, aware that in this strange world, not even princes were wholly safe.

His eyes were quizzical, faintly amused.

"Why not? Are you concerned for my safety, Emily? I find that touching," he said. "It might interest you to know that all this I have just said to you, I have told to no one else. So if my words come back to me, I shall know who has betrayed me."

Emily's face flamed. He had filled her with a breathless excitement coupled with humility, by confiding in her, and now he brought her down to earth by insinuating that she might betray him.

"I should not do that," she said stiffly. "I do not make a habit of revealing things told to me in confidence. If you have doubts about my dependability, then why speak to me about matters of such great importance?"

He fixed her with a slow, brooding stare. "Then to whom should I talk?" he asked. "In my way, Emily, I am as much alone here as you are. Minions falling at my feet, every desire accorded, but no one with whom to share an honest exchange of opinions." He smiled suddenly, his expression relaxed. "Look at you . . . you are thinking, here is this abominable fellow, trying to play on my sympathy again. Are you not? Shall we simply say that I am relying on your British sense of fair play?"

And once again, he left her mystified, not sure if he were serious or half-mocking, and totally at a loss to understand her own feelings. He had opened up to her, freely and completely, about his hopes and fears for the future of Bilkhondar, and yet he never came to her room without the two silent and formidable armed guards. Sometimes he spoke to her in a relaxed and friendly manner, especially when they were deeply involved in some shared interest, but even then, he could quite abruptly become remote and formal. And at other times, he could be savagely ironic and hurtful, as if he found her mere presence an imposition and an embarrassment.

For herself, all she knew for certain was that his visits had become the central pivot of her existence, she anticipated them with a mixture of pleasure and dread, never sure which of these contrary aspects of himself he would reveal. The life she had once known in England receded steadily from her, she thought of it less often and, she realised guiltily, with less regret, as she became more immersed in the present moment.

But this was such a gradual process that at first she could not chart its passage. It was an inching up and seeping away, slow and unmarked, the way the tide creeps up the shore, stealthily and unnoticed, until all at once there comes a point at which the extent of its encroachment is appreciated.

For Emily, too, this point was reached one day, a day that sliced like a great dividing line between the old life and the new, so that looking back, it was this she remembered, not the shipwreck nor the day she arrived in Bilkhondar, as the point of no return.

She was in her room one morning, dressed in the loose robe she wore on rising. Gulal was preparing her bath, and Yasmin brushing her hair, when the door burst open and Simone rushed unceremoniously in. The French girl was in a state of high excitement.

"Quickly, *Emilie!*" she cried out in the French they still used to converse privately between themselves. "You must come, but at once! Never again will you have a chance like this!"

Her agitation conveyed itself to Emily, who jumped to her feet.

"What is it, Simone?"

"British soldiers – in the courtyard!" Simone said breathlessly. "A new colonel has arrived at the garrison and has come to pay his respects to Prince Murad, so Qadir Bibi Bano says."

She seized Emily's hand and almost pulled her from her room, along the corridor to the gallery with the lattice grille overlooking the courtyard, and there, far below, Emily was in time to see a detachment of British officers, led by a full colonel, dismount from their horses.

"What are you waiting for?" hissed Simone. "If you really want to get out of here, the time is now!"

Emily gazed down at the brightly uniformed figures of her countrymen, and knew that freedom was suddenly and unbelievably within her grasp. She had only to raise her voice and shout, loudly and in English, and her presence would be discovered. They would turn their heads and see her, unmistakably English with her fair hair, and they would demand her release. And she did not seriously believe that any reprisals would be taken against her in the harem, to punish her indiscretion, for the finding of her dead body would cause more of an affray than would that of her live one.

Knowing all this, aware that it was in her power to bring about her release from this place, and her return to her own people, Emily stood, rooted to the spot, her hands clasped together, overcome by the realisation that she could not do it. Because to be taken away from Bilkhondar meant that she would never again see Prince Dara, and that she could not envisage.

She would rather endure the dangers and restrictions of life in the harem, the agony of each day's waiting for his visit, unsure of what it might mean. Because I love him, she thought helplessly, and even though I am nothing to him but a friend to talk to, a companion to fill his empty hours, and a victim for his occasional ill-humour, I would rather have that, than never to see him again, or hear his voice, or look into his eyes.

She turned her back on the courtyard. Without rancour, without regret, and with only a little shrug of resignation, Emily Hunter chose a life of imprisonment in the harem quarters of the Palace of Bilkhondar.

Simone, who had followed all this intently, saw the English girl's thoughts written plainly on her face.

"You are in love with him, aren't you?" she said. "What else would keep you here, when you could be free? Ah well, it is what I have suspected for some time."

"But how could you?" Emily cried. "I have only just realised the truth myself. Is it so obvious?"

"Only to me, because I have experience in such matters. I have seen this begin to happen to you, *chérie*, unbeknown to yourself, because, I think, you have never been in love before."

Emily shook her head, bewildered by the strength of her newly-discovered feelings.

"Never!" she cried. "I never imagined it could be like this!" A new thought occurred to her, and she said brokenly, "Forgive me, Simone. I have thrown away your chance of freedom along with my own. I had no right to do that."

The French girl's shoulders rose in a gesture of disdain.

"Pooh! Do not even think of it! Why should I wish to leave here, where I have ease and comfort and luxury, to be again some memsahib's servant, or to marry some poverty-stricken man who would make me old before my time? I am much happier here, believe me."

Emily looked at her friend's face and realised she was sincere in what she said. Simone was not oppressed by the restrictiveness of the harem as she, Emily, had been, because she had not been born to leisure or wealth; for her, life had only meant work and servitude of one kind or another.

Her mind returned to her own dilemma, and horrified, she asked, "You don't think that he knows – Prince Dara?"

"I doubt it. He has experience of women, but not of women such as you, who hide their real emotions behind a mask of cold politeness. But do you not wish him to know? He would be enchanted!"

"Absolutely not!" Emily declared emphatically. "He would be amused, possibly even a little embarrassed. Oh, I am well enough to talk to, since he has no one else who knows the world outside this place, but I mean nothing to him, and I should die of shame if he were to suspect how I feel."

And now her position was doubly ironic, for here she was, believed by everyone to be Prince Dara's favourite, installed in luxury and accorded every respect, and not only was this a charade, but she was no longer grateful for the fact. And she had no idea how to cope with this strange and overpowering emotion.

"Oh lyric love, half angel and half bird – and all a wonder and a wild desire." Was this what Browning had meant, this madness which cast her mind and senses into confusion? There was joy in seeing him enter her room, but she had to suppress that joy for all she was worth. And when she recoiled as if burned from the merest, unintentional touch of his hand, it was no longer because she feared him, but because she dared not let him see how deeply it affected her. So she withdrew from him, as far as she reasonably could, her heart beating so fast she was surprised he could not hear it.

She knew that somehow she must learn to be relaxed in his presence. She must achieve a measure of self-control, so that she could meet his eyes without having to look away in confusion, and speak to him without stumbling over her words. For if she continued to be tense and jumpy, he might become bored with her conversation, might find her company disagreeable, and simply stop coming. Without his visits, Bilkhondar would not be bearable, life itself would have no meaning. She must endeavour to be calm and pleasant, so that he found some reward in her friendship. Otherwise, she would lose even that, and it was all she could hope for.

With this in mind, having given herself a stern talking to, she really tried, that evening, to be agreeable and at the same time self-possessed, and almost convinced herself that she was succeeding, since she could not see the tight little smile on her own face.

He had brought her a book of Persian verses to help her practise what the tutor had taught her. Emily had an aptitude for learning languages, and had progressed rapidly, but the book was old, the script complex and elaborate, and she hesitated a little, unable to make it out.

"You are doing very well," he encouraged her. "I know it is difficult, but try it once more." He came and stood behind her, one slim hand on the curved back of the couch, the other on the page she was attempting to read.

The dark head and the fair one were so close as to be almost touching, so close that if she had lifted her face just a fraction, she was sure he could not fail to see the desperate longing in her eyes, the need for him to bend his head and kiss her as she so badly wanted to be kissed. Emily's nervous fingers let go of the book; it fell to the ground with a thud, and with it went the last vestige of her self-control.

She jumped up, turning her back on him, her face to the wall, her hands clutching madly at the priceless tapestries with their colourful lords and ladies.

She felt rather than saw him rise and stand behind her, quite close, but not touching her.

"Emily," he said. "Turn round – look at me." He did not raise his voice, there was no need. Two hundred years of Mogul authority spoke through him, and a short spell of Western education had not seriously impaired the habit of expecting obedience. Emily did as he asked, and looked into the fine eyes which regarded her levelly.

"Since you have been in Bilkhondar," he said, slowly and precisely, "have I in any way mistreated you, hurt you, molested you, or given you any reason to think that I might do any of these things?"

She did not reply, and he simply stood there, pinning her to the wall with his calm, authoritative gaze.

"I am prepared to wait," he said, with calm insistence. "You *will* answer me."

She saw that he had no intention of letting the matter drop until she had answered the question. "No," she said in a low voice. "You have not."

"Then why is it," he demanded, "that you jump like a scared rabbit every time I come near you? I am not a monster, Emily. Do you seriously believe I am going to attack you?"

Emily blinked furiously to prevent the tears springing to her eyes. Not five minutes ago, the effect of his nearness upon her had been so profound that she had feared she might throw herself into his arms, and embarrass both him and herself beyond any recovery of their friendship. She could not tell him that. He had not asked her to fall in love with him, had not sought this intense emotional response from her, nor in any way indicated that she held the slightest attraction for him.

She squared her shoulders, remembered reading somewhere that attack was the best method of defence, and resolved to bluff her way out of this impasse. Her pride, at least, would be intact.

"How am I to know what to believe?" she countered. "You have treated me with every consideration, it is true, but each time you come into this room, they are with you." She pointed at the two guards. "How can one be natural and unconstrained, with two enormous men with sharp swords forever standing guard at the door?"

"They serve a purpose," he said. "One simply pretends they are not there – like wallpaper. Don't try to tell me you do not have servants in England, and are not accustomed to their presence?"

"Our servants are not armed," Emily said drily.

"And we did not carry on our private business in front of them."

Dara's mouth twitched.

"Indeed. *Pas devant les domestiques*," he observed, and went on, entertained but not at all convinced by her digression. "You wish me to think it is my guards who make you nervous, but I don't believe that, Emily, not entirely. I think it is I myself, and I want to know why this should be. I have asked nothing from you but a civilised and undemanding friendship."

Resentment flared in Emily's eyes.

"And that is why I am installed here in this – this elegant brothel!" she burst out indignantly, "perfumed and scented and adorned to high heaven every day, with the slave-girls, and the other women, the eunuchs, everyone in the harem believing that I am your . . . that I am . . ." she faltered, unwilling to put it into words.

She saw anger blaze a swift trail across the Prince's handsome features, but his voice was cold and scornful when he spoke.

"So it is mere harem gossip which is the cause of your pique?" he said. "I have placed you in an untenable position, because all of these silly women believe I am making love to you, whereas, in fact, I am not? And they have groomed and prepared you for the role of favourite, have they not, in best seventeenth-century tradition?"

Very deliberately, with exaggerated formality, he bent and picked up the book she had dropped, and handed it to her, careful to avoid all possibility of their fingers touching.

"You may rest assured," he said icily, "that so long as you remain under this roof, you have nothing to fear from me. I do not make a practice of forcing my attentions on reluctant and frightened women who make it clear they would find such attentions repugnant. The very idea is distasteful to me."

He turned away from her, abruptly and with finality, and strode out of the room, followed closely by the stern-faced guards, leaving Emily standing where he had left her, clasping the book of Persian verse in her hands, tears running, unchecked, down her face.

That night she scarcely slept at all. The muezzin's call found her wide-eyed and unrested, and for most of the day she could not settle, or even sit in one spot for longer than a few minutes, plagued by the knowledge that she had angered and insulted him, and the terrible fear that he would never come near her again. She lived, minute by minute, towards the hour when he usually arrived, her ear straining for his now familiar footsteps, and the excitement he generated within the harem. But he did not come, and as time passed, it became apparent that he was not going to.

"You have quarrelled, eh?" Simone said knowledgeably. "Ah well, a quarrel is better than indifference. He will see you with different eyes tomorrow."

"He will not come tomorrow," Emily said dully. "I don't think he will ever come again."

"Bah!" Simone said dismissively. "I know men. You are different, and you intrigue him. He will come."

"He finds me distasteful." Emily grimaced at the word, and Simone glanced sharply at her.

"Then either he does not have eyes in his head, or you have handled the whole business appallingly," she said. Seeing Emily's eyes fill with tears, she added soothingly, "Don't cry. I'm sure it is not that bad."

She went to the door and called briskly, "Gulal! Bring some fruit. And send in Yasmin to light the lamps."

"Never mind the fruit. I'm not hungry," Emily insisted.

"I know. You have touched nothing all day. If you do not eat, tomorrow you will be bad-tempered, your head will ache, and if he comes, you will quarrel once more. But if you think it is of no consequence. . . ." She shrugged, but Emily saw her motion to the slave-girl to leave the basket of fruit. It was luscious, as it always was, and she knew Emily could seldom resist it.

Alone, Emily played a little desultory music on the pianoforte, gave it up and attempted to read a book. There was no joy in any of these things which usually pleased her, because the very centre of her world was awry. She picked idly at the fruit, ate one or two of the huge, golden grapes, and even that palled. She retired to bed and fell into an unhappy sleep.

In the middle of the night, she awoke with a searing agony, like fire in her guts. Her whole body seemed aflame, and yet she was shivering convulsively. Her head spun when she attempted to sit up. She screamed for Simone, and the French girl was there almost at once.

"What is it, *chérie*?"

"I don't know . . . pain, here!" Emily clutched her stomach, rolled over, hugging herself tightly, moaned helplessly as the pain gripped her once more.

By now, the whole corridor was awake, the slave-girls hovering anxiously in the doorway. Simone sent one of them scurrying to fetch Qadir Bibi Bano.

The Lady Protectress was swift and efficient. Her presence stilled the agitation among the women, which threatened to become hysteria. Her orders were calm, precise, and instantly obeyed. Vast quantities of liquid were forced down Emily's throat, and then as Qadir Bibi Bano supported the weight of her body, and

Simone held her head over a basin, she was induced to vomit, which she did, copiously, until her slender frame was exhausted by the effort. Then she was washed and put to bed, completely worn out, but out of danger.

She opened her eyes and gazed up at Qadir Bibi Bano.

"What's wrong with me?" she asked weakly.

"Nothing, now, that rest will not put right," the older woman replied, but Emily knew her grave, unsmiling expression well enough by now to recognize the concern behind it.

"But something was? Was it something I ate?"

"Almost certainly. You have been poisoned."

"Poisoned?" Emily struggled vainly to sit up, then fell back helplessly. "Deliberately poisoned? But that's ridiculous! Who would want to do that to me?"

In her bewilderment, she had lapsed into English. Simone materialised out of the shadows, and with some effort, Emily rephrased her questions in French.

"Here, it is not ridiculous, it is commonplace," Simone said, darkly. "You ate nothing today, but perhaps the fruit?"

Emily nodded. "And very little of that."

"It is as well — or you would now very surely be dead," said Simone. "The fruit has been examined. It contains enough poison to kill a roomful of us. Did I not tell you," she added, "that this is not a children's playground?"

Emily turned her head away. Someone wished her dead. She, Emily Hunter, who to the best of her recollection had never seriously hated anyone, she who was surely insignificant, unimportant. Someone had tried to kill her. I don't believe it, she whispered to herself before tiredness overcame her and she fell asleep.

Some time later, she awoke briefly and saw, or dreamed she saw, Dara sitting by her bed. He saw her eyelids flutter, and reached for her hand; the touch of his fingers was warm and real, but in the morning she was alone.

As always, the sun was shining. Simone bustled in, and smiled as she saw that Emily was awake.

"*Bonjour!* You feel better? Qadir Bibi Bano has given orders that you eat very lightly today, so there is not much in the way of breakfast for you."

Emily sat up. Apart from a little weakness and light-headedness, she felt almost normal, for which, once again, she could thank her robust constitution as much as the prompt action of Qadir Bibi Bano.

"I dreamed Prince Dara was here," she said.

Simone regarded her thoughtfully. "That was no dream," she said. "This man who finds you distasteful was at your bedside for most of the night. We have orders to let him know at any time, should your condition worsen. But you are going to get well. You are clearly stronger than you look."

Emily gave a rueful smile.

"Whatever he may think of me, he does not wish me dead," she said. "But who does, Simone? What have I done to anyone here, to make them hate me so much?"

The French girl shook her head.

"Not hatred – jealousy," she said. "It is not what you have done, but who you are, what you are believed to be. There is someone who thinks she should be in your shoes."

"Tell me, Simone," Emily insisted. "Someone has tried to kill me, and I have the right to know what it is all about."

"I agree, and so I will tell you, even though, when you came, we were all warned by Qadir Bibi Bano to say nothing of this to you, and at the time, I too thought it best you did not know."

She sat on the edge of Emily's bed.

"When Prince Dara was still a child, a marriage was arranged for him, by his father, with the daughter of an Indian prince whose territory adjoins Bilkhondar, although it is ruled by the British. Forget about your Queen Victoria and her beloved Albert. Here it is the custom for royal marriages to be contracted purely for dynastic or political reasons. I believe the father of this princess gave Prince Murad an undertaking to hold the frontier, should the British attempt to enter Bilkhondar that way. In return, his daughter eventually becomes the wife of a ruling prince."

Emily was silent for a few minutes, digesting the painful knowledge that this man she loved had a wife already chosen for him.

"Go on," she said.

"*Eh bien*. Prince Dara arrives back from England to find the Princess Jani and her entourage already here in Bilkhondar, awaiting an immediate marriage. The Prince has never met the girl before, and it is rumoured he is unwilling to plunge into marriage with a stranger, so asks his father for time. Prince Murad says the marriage must take place within the year, or her father will be insulted, demand the girl back, and declare the agreement null and void."

"And where is this princess now?" Emily forced herself to ask.

"She is here, inside the harem, in her own private apartments from which she never ventures, but nevertheless, she is almost certainly responsible for what happened to you last night. She is a proud, vindictive woman, determined to have what she feels is hers by right."

Emily gave a little sigh of bewilderment. In spite of her brush with death, in spite of Simone's warnings, she found it difficult to feel any fear. She knew she was still plain Emily Hunter from Overhampton, notwithstanding all the fine trappings of her present life, and it was unreal and slightly ridiculous to imagine anyone going to so much trouble to dispose of her.

"It is all a great fuss over very little," she said bluntly. "I am in no way preventing Prince Dara's marriage to the Princess, and she has little reason to be envious of me."

"*She* does not know that," Simone pointed out. "All she knows is that Prince Dara has installed you here in these rooms, where he spends many hours in your company. She draws her own conclusions from that, as does everyone else. He *must* marry her eventually, whether his heart is in it or not, for a betrothal, here, is as binding as a marriage, and cannot be cast aside easily. Do not dismiss this matter lightly, Emily, for this woman will not allow herself to be slighted, and your life is of no great consequence to her."

The arrival of Qadir Bibi Bano prevented any further discussion on the subject. The Lady Protectress was visibly relieved to see her charge restored to health, and although Emily knew Qadir Bibi Bano's own influence and prestige would suffer if someone was poisoned under her very nose, she was touched by the older woman's solicitude, and thanked her for acting so promptly and efficiently to save her.

"It was nothing. I could see at a glance what was wrong with you," she said briskly. "But we shall have to be doubly careful now. That little wretch Gulal, who brought you the fruit, she shall have the task of tasting everything before it reaches you."

Emily shuddered with revulsion at the notion of anyone's having to risk death on her behalf.

"Do not worry. I doubt the same trick will be played twice," Qadir Bibi Bano said grimly. "And she will be thankful to have been let off so lightly. Prince Dara is a different manner of man from his father. Had it been Prince Murad who was concerned, her fate would have been interrogation, torture and death."

Emily was on her feet, deeply agitated. "But you can't think Gulal was to blame!" she cried. "What nonsense! Where is she?"

Qadir Bibi Bano clapped her hands, and the girl, who must have been waiting behind the door, rushed in and flung herself at Emily's feet, sobbing loudly and protesting her innocence, still half expecting some terrible punishment to fall upon her.

"Oh, do get up! This is all too silly!" Emily said, lifting the weeping, red-eyed girl to her feet. "Please go now, and prepare my bath, and let us hear no more about it."

When Gulal was out of earshot, Qadir Bibi Bano said, "The Prince questioned her himself, and was satisfied she knew nothing. Her distress was too natural to be feigned by one so simple, and the fruit could have been tampered with at any stage on its progress from the kitchens. Still, guilty or not, Prince Murad would have made an example of her, if only to frighten off any other would-be murderers."

"That's horrible!" Emily declared. "Prince Dara would never do that."

"I know," said the Lady Protectress, and her eyes were grave as they met Emily's. "For that reason, he himself must walk with care, and so must all those of us who love him."

CHAPTER
FIVE

EMILY spent most of the day resting, and by evening was fully recovered. She had her hair brushed until it shone like gold, and put on a sari of palest apricot, shot through with golden thread, which picked up and reflected the lights in her hair. In spite of that ill-fated last meeting, the memory of which she found most painful, she knew she was clinging to the faint hope that he would come to see her, if only to discover for himself that she was well. It seemed an age since his last visit, and she was longing for the sight of him, even though he might still be cold and hostile towards her. Love makes fools of the most sensible of us, she thought ruefully, and wondered why it had been her destiny to fall in love with this man who did not desire her, and could never be hers.

But there was no mistaking the fierce, upward surge of her heart as she heard those footsteps in the corridor, and it was doubly hard to remain calm and hide the joy she felt as once again he entered her room, the guards close at his heels.

"Good evening, Your Highness," she said, in what she hoped was a cool but pleasant voice.

Prince Dara left the guards at the door and crossed the room to where she stood. Whatever might have passed between them on his previous visit, she saw clearly that it was no longer of any concern to him. All the anger and contempt, all the harsh words they had exchanged, were dismissed as mere trivialities in the face of what had happened to her. It was worth it, she thought, all the agony and pain, and almost dying, to see anxiety instead of scorn in the fine dark eyes.

"Believe me, Emily," he said, "I would not have had this happen to you for all the world."

"There is no need for Your Highness to worry," she said, almost insouciantly. "I am quite well again. I must take more care, that's all."

He shook his head. "If only it were so simple," he said. "This was no accident, Emily."

"I know all about it, and who was responsible," she said, finding herself strangely calm, and anxious only to reassure him.

He sighed. "Do you? It was inevitable, I suppose, that you should find out about *her*. But it does not matter, now, because there is only one solution to the problem, and I intend to find it."

She looked up at him, her blue eyes full of questions.

"Don't you realise," he said quietly, "the dilemma I have been in, ever since you arrived here? I know it is wrong for a young English lady of your background and upbringing to be kept here in the harem of a court that still lives in feudal times. The knowledge has tormented me, and made me feel personally guilty, and responsible for your fate."

"But you did not –" she interrupted, and he silenced her with a swift gesture of his hand.

"No, I did not, but I have gone along with the situation, and see what has happened. You were nearly killed last night. Your father gave his life to save yours – the fishermen found you tied to the lifebelt with his neck-cloth – and here, in my country, in my palace, a jealous woman tried to kill you, through no fault of your own. It cannot go on like this, Emily, I shall not permit it."

They gazed at one another across the few feet of space that separated them, the Prince and the girl from England, cast together by such unlikely circumstances. Her eyes were wide and serious.

"What will you do?" she whispered.

"Listen to me. Take no notice of them –" he nodded towards the guards, "– they don't understand English and have no idea what we are talking about. I am going to get you out of here. It will require subterfuge, we shall have to disguise you and smuggle you out of the harem. I will work out the details of it and send you a message. Once outside the palace, I have friends amongst the hill tribes, and they can take you over the border to the garrison in British India. You will be safe there. My father will not be pleased when he finds out," he shrugged resignedly, "but I am his only son, and I think I can mollify him."

Emily heard almost nothing of the latter part of his speech. All she registered was that he intended engineering her escape from Bilkhondar, and that was sufficient to set all her senses in a panic. He was planning to send her away, to where she would never see him again. She would have to endure the rest of her life without him, and the thought of it was more than she could bear.

She forgot her pride and her caution, it ceased to matter whether he wanted her here, or whether he cared for her at all – she had to be near him, at whatever cost.

Emily covered the physical space between them in seconds, and in her distraction, broke through the barriers that had kept her for so long at arm's length from him. She seized his hands in hers and cried, "No, Dara, please don't sent me away!"

He was looking down at her, his eyes dark with amazement, and she, unaware in her intense agitation that for the first time she had spoken his name, was still clinging fiercely to him, almost sobbing out her desperation.

"I won't be any trouble to you, I'll just live here quietly in the harem, only don't send me away, because I love you so much, and I don't believe I can live without you, not now!"

She tore her gaze from him and stared wretchedly at the blue and rose flowers on the carpet, leaving him looking down at the top of her bowed golden head.

"Is this true?" he asked, softly but incredulously. She nodded dumbly, and he lifted her chin with his hand, so that her eyes met his once more. She had no need to speak, for he saw in her unguarded eyes all the need, all the longing she had fought to suppress.

"Leave us!" he ordered the guard, and, their expressions unchanging, they retired to the corridor. For the very first time since they met, Emily and Prince Dara were alone together.

A wry smile touched the corners of his mouth as he lifted both her hands to his lips.

"I should not have done that," he said. "Those guards have been there for your protection. I dared not be alone with you, because I have loved you from the first moment I came into this room and saw you there, looking so frightened and yet so resolute. My dearest Emily, my beloved."

The eyes she raised to his were shining now, radiant with joy, as he drew her closer to him. Holding her in the circle of his arms, he bent and kissed her, a kiss that was at the same time tender and passionate. Emily felt her whole being melt into his, as if all her life had been moving inexorably towards this exquisite moment. The guards outside the door, the busy quarters of the harem and all the world beyond, had ceased to exist for the space of those few heartbeats – there was nothing beyond the rapturous wonder of being in his arms.

When at last his lips released hers, she rested her head against his chest, where she could feel the strong beat of his heart.

"My darling, let us have no more talk of sending me away," she begged. "You cannot smuggle me out of the harem against my wishes, and I promise you, I will not go. I will scream so loudly the whole palace will hear me!"

For an answer, he bent and lifted her bodily into his arms.

"All that was long ago, before you kissed me, before I dreamed that you could love me," he said fervently. "For you and me, nothing can ever be the same again. Don't you know that?"

Still carrying the smiling and radiant girl in his arms, Prince Dara strode across the room to the bedchamber, brushing aside the silken hangings which fell softly back into place, an unheeded cascade of glorious colour, behind them.

In the morning, when Emily stirred and opened her eyes, Dara was sitting on the edge of the bed already fully dressed, and in the process of fastening the cummerbund around his tunic.

She blinked, and stretched both arms luxuriously above her head. It was very early, for the sun had not risen, and the room was still half dark.

"You are not leaving?" she asked

"I must, dearest. My father rises early and he will expect me in his hall of private audience before he attends the jharoka."

He bent and brushed a lock of tangled hair from her eyes, kissed her forehead and then her lips, slowly and lovingly. She clasped both her hands at the back of his neck, as if she might physically prevent him from going.

"I will be back this evening," he promised. "Nothing will keep me from you now."

"A day – a whole day without you!" she complained, only half-jokingly, crisping her fingers through the shining black hair. "How much time we have already wasted, you and I, Dara! I thought you did not care for me, that I was unattractive to you."

"You were all I could desire," he told her, "but you were not a harem woman, who knows and accepts what is expected of her, that she is here to be taken. How could I treat you as if you were? How could I make love to you when you recoiled from me as if you found me monstrous?"

"I *was* afraid of you in the beginning," she confessed, "before I knew you. And then, when I knew that I loved you, it was only my stupid pride which made me behave that way."

He detached her hands gently from around his neck, and sat regarding her thoughtfully.

"In a way, your pride was right," he said. "You have given yourself to me without reserve, and I can give you nothing in return, except my love. You know, don't you, that I am not free to marry you? Not only that, but one day I must marry the Princess Jani?"

She shook her head impatiently, as if to ward off this unpleasant thought.

"I know it, but please don't let us talk about it – not

this morning," she said. "I want only your love, nothing more."

He gathered her into his arms again, and held her tightly. "You have that, now and always, whatever happens," he said steadily. "My love and my protection, with my life if necessary."

He let her go, reluctantly, and got to his feet.

"I have to go now, beloved. I have given instructions to those who wait on you that they must be more vigilant than ever before. You, too, must take care. Never forget for a minute that there is danger here."

When he had gone, Emily lay still and quiet for a while, her mind reliving, joyfully and incredulously, the night they had spent together. She was a woman, now, in every sense of the word. He had made her a new heaven and a new earth, she knew love and passion and ecstasy, and now she could only echo what he had said to her – nothing could ever be the same again. With a little smile of happiness on her face, Emily drifted off to sleep, and that was how Simone found her, some hours later.

"His Highness was here the entire night," whispered Yasmin. "Before he left, he instructed me to remain awake outside the door until morning. How he loves her!" The girl sighed deeply.

Simone cast her a sharp look.

"Of course he loves her – everyone is aware of that, even she herself, at last!" she muttered. "Be about your business, girl, and see to it that when you are outside that door at night, you stay awake!"

The world Emily now lived in was utterly changed, or so it seemed, although in reality it remained the same – it was she who had changed. The gardens and pavilions and halls of the harem, which she had once thought of as a prison, had become a paradise, since she no longer had any desire to be anywhere else. Here was the man she loved, who also, incredibly, loved her, and all she needed was to be with him. In him she had everything, she was totally fulfilled. England was almost a forgotten dream, and the rest of India might not have existed; her life was here.

"I never dreamed that there could be happiness such as this," she said. "I cannot help but feel that it is all too perfect, that it cannot last. That we shall have to suffer for it."

"My love, you must not think that," he urged her. "it is merely your puritanical English upbringing which has left you with this sense of . . . what does one call it?"

"Retribution," Emily said grimly.

"You must forget this idea. We are not sinners. I love you, you love me, and it is not wrong to love. We have been given something beautiful, and we should accept it gratefully, and not ask too many questions. We did not ask for this to happen to us, Emily, both of us fought against it, and it defeated us. What can we do against such a force?"

He was right, she knew. The love she felt for him had carried her too far and too swiftly, there was no alternative but to go on loving him, whatever it cost her. But there was a shadow over her happiness: the Princess Jani, whom he must one day marry, who, from the seclusion of her quarters, had already made one attempt on Emily's life, and who waited, like some unseen and brooding presence, for what she believed was rightfully hers.

Emily had been perfectly sincere when she told Dara that to have his love would be enough, but she would have been less than human had she been sanguine about the idea of him married to the other girl.

"You say you love me, and I believe you, but will you be so sure when you are married to *her*? Will you have to lie with her . . . to do all the things we do?"

"The marriage will have to be consummated, yes," he agreed guardedly. "Which is not exactly the same as you said."

Emily's mind did a sudden, unpredictable flashback to a scene in their drawing-room at Overhampton a year or two earlier, when she had overheard her mother's guests discussing the scandal of the writer John Ruskin, whose wife was seeking a divorce on grounds of non-consummation. They had changed the subject the minute they realised she was in the room, and the sixteen-year-old girl, totally untutored sexually, had been left to herself to work out what was meant by this fascinating word.

"That's a polite way of saying you will be taking another woman to bed," she said, sadly and a little angrily.

He said patiently, "You must not distress yourself over it. It will mean nothing to me."

She thought of her own experience, and said incredulously, "How can it mean nothing?"

"Oh, I promise you it can," he assured her. "It can be everything – or nothing at all. You think it will be as it is for you and me?" He shook his head. "Never, Emily. I shall consummate the marriage. I shall not make love to her."

"It is a fine distinction."

"But a very real one. You should pity this woman, even while you beware of her jealousy, because she will have only the empty title and the empty shell. *You* will always be the one I love."

With that she had to be content, and since, at the

moment, it was all hypothetical, she managed, most of the time, to be so.

He gave her, although he never used it privately, the name of Nadira, because it meant "the Excellent" and because, so he told her, it had been the name of the first Prince Dara's consort. More often, he compared the two of them to Shah Jehan and Mumtaz Mahal, the woman for whom he had built the Taj, although she had been a princess, and his wife. He, too, had contracted other marriages for political reasons, but he had loved always and only her, and had been heartbroken when she died young, bearing the last of their fourteen children.

Emily shivered when she heard this story.

"Don't talk of death," she begged. "I don't relish the idea of dying, but I think it would be preferable to losing you."

"I am young and healthy, and not planning immediately to die," he said, laughing, "although one must always be prepared. Remember the lines we were reading the other day – Christina Rossetti, was it not?

> 'When I am dead, my dearest,
> Sing no sad songs for me;
> Plant thou no roses at my head
> Nor shady cypress tree.'

The poet seems to be saying that we are free to forget the one who is gone."

"Ah," she rejoined, "but I prefer the sentiments expressed by the same poet,

> 'Remember me when I am gone away,
> Gone far away into the silent land –' "

They looked at each other in silence, as if gripped by a strange and eerie presentiment.

"I could never, ever forget," she protested fervently. A sense of the shortness, the transience of life, was upon them, and he pulled her into his arms with a new intensity.

It must have been soon afterwards that she noticed a change in the rhythm of her life that had been essentially the same, month after month, since the beginning of her adolescence. Furthermore, she had short bouts of nausea which briefly incapacitated her in the mornings, and it was following one of these that Simone sent for Qadir Bibi Bano, who inspected Emily cursorily, and then beamed on her with unprecedented approval.

"You are with child," she told her bluntly. "It is good, of course. As the mother of Prince Dara's child, your future is more secure. But we shall have to be even more watchful, for when *she* finds out, her envy will know no bounds."

Emily said, "But are you sure about this?"

"I have seen these signs too often to be other than sure," she asserted confidently. "In a little while, you will feel the child move, and then you will know for yourself. Do not look so surprised. Surely you knew this could happen?"

Yes, Emily supposed, vaguely she had been aware that it could, she had simply never thought about it. She laid a hand on her stomach, still smooth and flat, and tried to imagine it distended in pregnancy, tried to imagine the real baby in her arms. The baby! Her heart contracted with excitement and tenderness. Her baby – his child!

She could not wait to tell him. It would have been more clever to wait for a suitable moment to impart such momentous news, but she was too eager and excited for cleverness, and as soon as they were alone, she seized both his hands, and burst out, "Dara, I am going to have a child!"

An expression of incredulous joy illuminated the handsome features; he picked her up and swung her into the air, and then bethought himself, and set her down on the divan with meticulous care.

"I should not have done that," he said apologetically, "but it is difficult to express in words how happy I am. We have so much, you and I."

"We don't have it yet," she reminded him, a flicker of apprehension clouding her thoughts. "Qadir Bibi Bano says about another six months. Dara, is there a doctor in Bilkhondar? A European-trained doctor, I mean?"

He shook his head, and now he, too, looked worried. "There is no doctor. Was I not saying to you, not so long ago, that we needed modern medicine? I did not dream, then, how soon we should need it."

"Then what happens when children are born here?" she whispered.

"There are women who understand about child-birth, and if things are straightforward, all is usually well. But there's no denying that the babies die, sometimes, and sometimes . . ." he stopped abruptly.

"Sometimes the mothers die, too," she finished, in a small voice. "So they do in England. I remember quite recently, a woman in the village. . . ." Something else suddenly struck her. "My mother lost her first child, and very nearly her life, in India. And after I was born, the doctors said it would be better if there were no more children."

With her newly-gained knowledge of life, Emily now saw another reason why her mother and father had found it politic to live apart, and now she had the maturity to pity her, rather than to apportion blame.

She herself had been healthy and strong all her life, but what if she had inherited her mother's tendency to have difficulty in bearing children?

She said as much to Dara, and he frowned and said decisively, "A doctor must be obtained for you. We have six months – it should be long enough to procure one from somewhere in India so that he may be here when the time comes."

"Will your father allow it?"

"That is our greatest problem. My father is strongly against permitting Europeans to visit his principality. They are inquisitive and pry into matters he believes are no one's concern but his own. What is more, they tend to bring change with them as part of their luggage, and change is something he cannot countenance. But do not fear, this is his first grandchild, and somehow he must be persuaded."

It was still so far in the future that Emily was able to put her apprehension aside, and if it were possible, it seemed that their joy in each other was increased by the knowledge of the coming event. Her bouts of sickness soon ceased, she felt fit and well, her hair and skin took on a new glow, and her figure an unprecedented voluptuousness.

Cocooned in happiness, sustained by Dara's love, she allowed herself, mistakenly, to drift into a state of complacent well-being and security. Simone and the slave-girls were solicitous, the few women in the harem whom she had got to know well at least gave the appearance of rejoicing in her good fortune. Even Qadir Bibi Bano relaxed her stern manner and did all she could to see that Emily was well cared for. Dara was consideration itself, even sending off to England for such delicacies as beef tea and calves-foot jelly, and she could not bring herself to tell him that by the time the things arrived, the craving for them had been replaced by one quite different.

Two things happened in rapid succession to shake her out of this illusion of safety. She awoke one night to an awareness of someone's being in the room. At first she thought it was simply the continuation of something she had been dreaming, but as she lay rigid in the darkness, the feeling would not go away, and the first prickings of fear made gooseflesh on her skin.

The door of her apartment had no lock – none of the inner apartments of the harem could be locked. For reasons of security and the implacable discipline of the harem, the inmates were not permitted absolute privacy. But one of the slave-girls kept watch outside Emily's door every night.

She sat up, slowly and carefully. Fitful moonlight shining in from the garden outlined the dark shapes of furniture, and she could just discern the bulk of the pianoforte.

"Who's there?" she called sharply, and in the stillness, she heard an unmistakable rustle of silk. Throat dry, pulse thudding, Emily felt for the floor with her feet, and that same instant, a solid human form flashed past her. She shot out a hand and grabbed wildly, and her fingers closed over the soft skin of a female arm.

Her quarry did not struggle, but stood facing her, and as her eyes began to see better in the gloom, Emily made out the shape of a woman, heavily veiled. From her garb she thought, for one blessed moment of relief, that it was Yasmin, who was on guard duty that night, but almost immediately, she sensed that it was not. The woman gave out menace as another might exude perfume, the signals were unmistakable.

"Who are you?" Emily gasped hoarsely. The intruder did not reply, and impelled by a primal instinct to know her adversary, Emily let go of the other woman's arm, reached up and pulled the veil from her face. A darkly beautiful visage, eyes glittering, sensuous mouth curved in a sardonic smile, regarded her for a fraction of a second, before its owner made the most of her advantage, and ran swiftly, her slippered feet making no sound, towards the door.

Emily pursued her as fast as she could, and was in time to see her midnight visitor turn the corner of the corridor. Even then, had she raised the alarm, she might have had her recaptured, but her attention was distracted by the sight of the unfortunate Yasmin, lying motionless on the floor, face downwards, an ugly gash on the back of her head staining her shining dark hair with blood.

She knelt down and gently turned the girl over, relieved to discover that though unconscious she was still breathing. She called for Simone, and together they carried the injured girl back into Emily's apartment, and laid her carefully on a divan. By the time Qadir Bibi Bano arrived, Emily had already begun to wash and clean the wound.

"Let me do that," the Lady Protectress said briskly. "It is not work for you."

"I am no stranger to the sickroom," Emily told her calmly. "I nursed my mother through her last illness, and I don't faint at the sight of blood."

"Maybe not, but in your condition it could easily turn your stomach, and on no account can we risk your losing the child." Qadir Bibi Bano took the basin and cloth in her capable hands. "This silly girl has much to answer for when she comes to her senses – as do we all. Once again, you could easily have been killed."

"What about her?" Emily demanded, indicating the still senseless Yasmin. "She almost was."

"*She* is not the chosen one of His Highness and the mother of his coming child," the older woman said contemptuously. "Her life would scarcely be missed amongst the thousands like her."

"It is nonetheless valuable to her," Emily pointed out. "Qadir Bibi Bano, I do not think it is right to hold these young girls responsible for my safety. You did not see the face of this woman who was in my room. Neither did I, very clearly, but there was no mistaking her hostility or her purpose. Yasmin was no match for her."

"I agree with you," she assented, regarding Emily with some respect. "From tomorrow night, two armed eunuchs will be posted outside your door. I myself will order this arrangement before consulting Prince Dara, for I am quite sure he will only confirm it."

Emily said, "Must the Prince be told of this? He will only be worried. Can't we spare him that?"

"That is quite impossible," Qadir Bibi Bano said firmly. "Even if I were to say nothing, other voices would tell him. Nothing appertaining to you can ever be kept secret from him."

Yasmin regained consciousness not long afterwards, but she was dazed and in pain, and soon fell asleep again. It was morning before she was able to tell them anything, and what she imparted was of little use. Yes, she had seen the girl coming towards her, but what was another slave-girl in the harem? Even during the night, messages could be sent, errands performed. It was unusual that the woman was veiled, within the harem confines, but not suffiently to arouse suspicion. She had walked quite slowly and normally past Yasmin, who had not turned to watch her progress; the next thing she knew was the blow on her head, and then nothing.

Dara came during the morning, which in itself was a break from their usual routine of life. He was dressed for riding, and stood gravely regarding the toe of his leather boot, whilst Emily gave him her version of the night's events.

He said, "Tell me one thing, Emily. In your opinion, who was this ill-intentioned intruder of yours?"

She said, "In spite of her slave-girl disguise, there is no doubt in my mind that this was the Princess Jani herself. I felt her hatred as clearly as I felt her breath on my face."

He frowned deeply.

"I was afraid so, and against her, personally, there is no action we can take. She is the bride chosen for me by my father, to whom I have been betrothed from my infancy. She is the future Crown Princess of Bilkhondar, and the treaty my father has with her father is, to him, more important than the life of any woman I happen to love."

He spoke bitterly. "Any complaint I take to him concerning her will be met by the response that I should redress her grievances by marrying her, as I was intended to do."

Emily said, "You cannot expect your father to care about my fate. I am nothing to him, only a plaything he acquired for your amusement, which has turned out to be rather tiresome."

"But to me you are more precious than life. Remember that," he said fiercely. "From now on, you will be guarded by armed eunuchs, as Qadir Bibi Bano has already arranged."

"Like a prisoner?" she said distastefully. "Just when I was beginning to feel that this was not a prison, but my home."

He sighed. "I know how onerous it must be to you, to

be so confined and guarded. I can only ask you to bear it – for my sake, if not for your own, knowing how much you mean to me, especially now."

Emily was closer to despair than she had been since her first traumatic days in the harem. Intrigue and treachery confronted her at every turn, and there seemed to be no way in which she could fight back against an enemy who was free to strike at will, and had the protection of the highest power in the land. She could only wait, never knowing when the next blow would fall, her only defence to be watched and guarded every waking and sleeping hour of her life.

"Is it always to be like this?" she cried out. "Is this the way my whole life must be lived? Armed guards outside my door, other people's lives at risk so that mine might be safe? How can I bear it, Dara? How can I?"

He said, "There is no other way for us, Emily. If we are to be together, we must face the dangers and combat them. This is Bilkhondar, and I cannot change it for you – not yet."

His words offered her no comfort, only the plain truth. He was too honest to gloss over the very real threat to her life, the powerful forces which strove to separate them, one way or another.

"I have made you pay too high a price for my love," he said soberly.

"Never," she said. Unconsciously, her back straightened, the light of battle came back into her eyes. "I did not mean what I said. I was just taken aback, momentarily, by all that has happened."

"As anyone would be," he conceded.

"Maybe. But I am all right now. Truly, I am."

He held her hand for a moment. "I knew you were too brave to give way completely to despair," he said.

"We shall win through, Emily, some day – because we must. The alternative is unthinkable. Until tonight." He kissed her, and then left her mulling over what he had said.

To have been accosted during the night, by a woman who wanted to kill her, was frightening enough, but Emily would have been unwise to believe that nothing worse could happen to her in this world of luxury and menace. She was relaxing in her room one day, reading a book, when Qadir Bibi Bano burst in, and Emily had never seen her so agitated. Her normally impassive face was strained and distorted with fear.

"You are in great danger, Excellent One," she said, in a low voice. "Prince Murad's personal guards are in the harem, and they have come to conduct you into the royal presence."

Emily's heart did a somersault of pure terror.

"What does Prince Murad want with me?" she whispered.

"How can I know? Within the harem, I may have power, but I am not permitted to question his authority, nor that of his messengers. They bear his seal, and I cannot prevent them from carrying out his orders. But I warn you – have a care how you speak, and how you behave. He has the power of life and death over you. In all my years here, I have never known a woman of the harem taken into his presence other than for the usual purpose, to return alive."

A deep shudder convulsed Emily's body, as the door was flung open without ceremony, and two of Prince Murad's guards strode in and seized her roughly by the arms.

Qadir Bibi Bano had time only to draw the girl's veil over her face and to whisper, "Have courage. I shall do the only thing I can for you – send word to Prince

Dara," before Emily was almost dragged out into the corridor.

The guards were immense and silent, and carried bare swords. They walked, one on either side of Emily, on a seemingly interminable journey, leaving behind the familiar halls and rooms of the world she knew, and traversing endless corridors, past doors she had never before been allowed to go through. They saw no one but the sinister black eunuchs and the male guards on the outer doors, but Emily knew that countless eyes followed their progress, she sensed the awed hush that pervaded the harem, the breathless consciousness of another's disaster which held it in collective suspense.

"They think I am going to my death," she thought morbidly, and on the heels of that idea came another, irresistibly, "Am I?" She had committed no crime, but did that matter, here, where there was no judicial process, where one man's word was law, and that man saw her as a trifling and annoying obstacle in the way of his plans?

Could she, Emily Hunter, face death? She had been so near to it, once in the shipwreck and twice more recently, here in the palace, but never quite like this, alone and without any defence, at the mercy of the will of another.

"You are too brave to give way to despair," Dara had said to her not long ago, but was she, she wondered brave enough to take this in a manner which would not shame her? She only knew that her stomach felt like water, and her legs were almost collapsing with fear as she walked.

At length she was brought to a vast chamber, whose only magnificence was in the splendid silver inlay of walls and ceiling and chased silver lamps. She had thought the room to be empty, but lifting her gaze, she saw, at the far end, a huge silver throne, upon which was seated an immobile figure.

The guards escorted her to the centre of the room, then halted, and automatically she did likewise, fixing her gaze upon the still distant figure on the throne.

"You – woman – will approach."

The voice was thin but penetrating, and spoke in precise, perfectly enunciated Persian. The selfsame authority she had noted in the son, only in him tempered by moderation and good humour, was here in the father in its purest form – sheer, unquestioned, dictatorial power.

Emily walked slowly and steadily, willing her steps not to falter, until she was within ten paces of the throne, then an imperious hand, ablaze with diamonds, forbade her to come closer. Prince Murad, absolute ruler of Bilkhondar, and Emily Hunter, late of Overhampton, faced each other for the first time.

She executed a neat curtsey, then rose to her feet again, and looked him straight in the face. Her fear had not left her, but she had made up her mind to hide it, for she knew, without being told, that this was a man who would show only contempt for timidity.

The proud, hawk-like visage appeared even more forbidding at close quarters than it had from the jharoka, the enormous diamond centrepiece of his silk turban dazzled her eyes. *His* eyes were hard and unyielding, without a trace of compassion in them.

"You will remove the veil from your face," he commanded.

Emily lifted the thin gauze to one side and let it fall, and Prince Murad subjected her to a long, fierce scrutiny.

"So this is the face of the one who has bewitched my son," he said distastefully. "By Allah, there are women more beautiful in this kingdom!"

She took a deep breath, and spoke slowly and clearly in Persian.

"I do not claim to be beautiful, although in my own country we have a saying that beauty is in the eye of the beholder," she said. "I love your son, as he loves me, but I have not bewitched him."

Prince Murad gave her a look of sharp surprise, as if impressed, despite himself, by her command of the language.

"Who gave you leave to speak?" he rapped. "You will be silent until ordered to reply, unless you desire your brazen head to be parted from your shoulders. Do you realise that I have only to give the word, for you to be instantly put to death?"

Emily said nothing, and Prince Murad hissed angrily, "Answer!"

"Your Highness had not given me leave to speak," she said sweetly. "But how could I not know that in Bilkhondar your word is law?"

He stared suspiciously at her, not disarmed, but intrigued to know what manner of woman this was, who answered back, albeit politely.

"My son is betrothed to a princess of ancient lineage," he said, his hard, brooding stare still fixed on Emily's face. "Her, he insults by his negligence, his reluctance to marry, whilst you, an infidel and a foreigner, claim his affections. My country cries out for a legitimate heir to the throne, and what is the news that is brought to my ears? The foreign woman is with child! *Is this true?*" thundered Prince Murad, pointing an angry finger at Emily.

"It is true, sire," she said quietly.

He lapsed into silence for a while, and she stood there, swaying a little, the effects of this prolonged ordeal beginning to tell. A slow, treacherous fatigue began to take possession of her, her strength ebbing away, and she wished that whatever he had a mind to do to her, he would get it over with. She wanted only to lie down and close her eyes, and be done with it all.

"Do not think," he castigated her, purring with malice, "that your condition, or my son's infatuation, will save you from my wrath. Insolent wretch! Have you no words to plead for your miserable life?"

Emily raised her eyes. With a tremendous effort of will, she stayed on her feet, and with her last ounce of spirit, aware that she might be signing her own death warrant, she answered him.

"I did not ask to be brought here, to be taken away from my own people and made a prisoner," she said bitterly. "You brought me here to please your son, and now you are angry with me because I have done so. I did not ask him to love me, but I am proud and happy that he does, and nothing will make me regret it. You may dispose of me as you wish, for no words of mine can prevent you."

Prince Murad sprang to his feet, too irate for speech. A wave of his hand signalled the guards, and at once, they took hold of Emily and dragged her to her knees. One of them pulled back her arms, and the other took her long hair in his hands and scraped it from her neck so harshly that the pain tore at her scalp. She saw the glint of his unsheathed sword and prayed silently, oh please, let it be quick, only let it be quick.

From some unknown resource deep within her, came a last, desperate ounce of courage. She refused to die permitting this tyrant to think her afraid. Flinging back her head, she stared at him defiantly.

Prince Murad stayed the guards with a brief gesture of his hand, slowly descended the steps from the dais and approached the girl. Pausing an arm's length away from her, he said, "Release the woman," and Emily was free of those terrible hands.

Looking down at her, the old despot who ruled Bilkhondar reached out and took a strand of Emily's hair in his hand.

"All my life I have respected courage," he said. "You have courage, like no woman I have ever seen before. You have beauty, too, of a sort," he added grudgingly. "And after all, you are carrying my grandson. Live, foreign woman, and pass on these qualities you possess to my son's child."

Emily was incapable of speech, the palms of her hands and her forehead were beaded with perspiration, she was weak with relief, and still only half aware of the narrow escape she had just experienced. She was still kneeling there helplessly when the ring of booted feet on the marble floor broke in on the tableau they presented.

"What is this? What's going on?" demanded Prince Dara's clear, angry voice, and then he was at Emily's side, lifting her to her feet, supporting her with his arm around her waist. "My poor love – are you hurt?" he asked, and she could only shake her head in reply.

Prince Murad's manner unbent visibly as he looked at his only surviving legitimate son.

"Your woman is unharmed, thanks to my forbearance, in spite of her insolence," he said.

Prince Dara looked steadily at his father. "Is this the honour of the Mogul line – to vent our spite on defenceless girls?"

"It ill becomes you to speak of honour, my son, when a royal princess, contracted to you in marriage, languishes here in this very palace, waiting for you to fulfil your obligation," said Prince Murad.

"A contract sealed without my knowledge or consent," Dara pointed out, "without any thought for my happiness."

Prince Murad spat contemptuously. "Happiness!" he said disgustedly. "Another of these foolish notions you have brought back from the land of the infidels, that man exists in order to be happy! I was wrong to have given in to your persuasions and sent you there. Take your happiness where you find it, but first, do your duty!"

Father and son stared at each other across a chasm of centuries. There was love and sadness in both their faces, one man locked in the grip of feudalism, the other on the brink of the modern world, striving vainly to make some kind of contact.

"Whatever your opinion on the value of happiness," said Dara, "it was to make me happy you had the Lady Nadira brought here, and since she has been here, I have enjoyed contentment I never knew before. You cannot deny this."

The stern visage permitted itself a brief smile. "This I freely admit. You were like a restless lion in a cage before, my son. I feared for your sanity."

"Now I am sane and content, and you have her to thank for that," said Dara. "Furthermore, she is going to bear my child, your grandchild. Yet twice during the last few weeks, her life has been threatened, and this very day she has been subjected to a frightening experience."

Prince Murad grunted. "Her fear was well concealed," he conceded grudgingly. "I grant you that she is courageous and exceedingly spirited. I have no objection to your keeping as many favourites as you require –

what else are women for? – so long as you do not neglect your duty."

He shrugged. "As for these little accidents in the harem . . . it is regrettable, but even I, omnipotent as I am, cannot have eyes everywhere."

Prince Dara smiled faintly, his arm tightened round Emily's waist, and it was clear he understood perfectly well what his father was saying. So long as the Princess Jani remained unwed, Emily's life was still in danger.

"Can we not achieve some kind of compromise?" he suggested.

Prince Murad dismissed the guards, and they retreated as far as the doors of the hall of audience, where they were out of range of normal conversation. Such inner diplomacy was not for their ears, and if he were about to give any ground, the old tyrant did not want it known that he had done so.

"What had you in mind, my son?" he said warily.

"Simply this. Let her be safe, let her be left in peace. Give me your word that she will not be in any danger, and that when her child is born, neither of them will be harmed. In return, I give you my word that within a week of the safe delivery of the child, I shall marry the Princess Jani."

Prince Murad stroked his chin thoughtfully, and his son added slyly, "I know it is in your power to guarantee her safety, since all in this kingdom can be ordained by you."

The ruling Prince gave the sigh of a man deeply put upon, but his eyes glinted with satisfaction.

"My word is given," he said.

"As is mine," replied his son. "Do I now have your permission to take the Lady Nadira back to her quarters?"

"You may take her where you will," his father said

dismissively, waving them from his presence. "And I shall hold you to your bargain!" he called shrilly after them.

Once again, the guards escorted them back to the harem, but this time they walked behind at a respectful distance, their swords sheathed. Emily clung tightly to Dara's arm, every step an effort, and after a short while he stopped, picked her up, and carried her inert, tired body the rest of the way to her apartments.

CHAPTER
SIX

EMILY recovered physically from her ordeal quickly enough, given rest and the ordered tranquillity of the harem routine, but she did not think, deep down, that she would ever forget the horrifying flash of those wicked swords, and the moment she had thought they were meant for her. She was still not sure if Prince Murad would have carried through his implicit threat to kill her.

Dara thought not.

"He wanted to scare you, to avenge himself on you and on me for having thwarted his plans."

She gave a short laugh.

"Then you have played into his hands, my love," she said sadly, "for you gave him your word you would marry, you even set a date."

"I had to," he said. "Don't you see that? We have not lost very much, you and I. We both knew I would have to marry some day; this only means I cannot continue to procrastinate indefinitely. This way I have guaranteed something vital to me – your life, yours and the baby's."

"Can you trust his word, and what is more to the point, can you trust Jani to abide by it?" she countered, unsure.

"Yes. My father is a crafty old tyrant, but he is strong on the concept of honour, as he perceives it. Besides, he is not stupid. I have agreed to do as he wishes. As for the

Princess, what she tried to do before must have had his tacit consent, although I doubt he and she have spoken together directly, on that subject or any other. But she will know that he has forbidden any further mishaps to your person, and she will not risk disobedience."

"Besides," Emily pointed out, wryly, "she will also know that soon she will be your wife, she has only to wait a few short months. And after you are married – then what?" She could not resist voicing the question which had been gnawing relentlessly at her mind.

"Then nothing. My father has not asked that I give you up, nor shall I. Nor would he expect it. My passions are, to him, my own affair, so long as I fulfil my duties. You and I, Emily, will be as we always have been."

"Will we? I wonder," she said. "I shall hate every minute you spend with her."

"I shall relish it no more than you. Try to see it for what it is – a matter of state, of politics, of protocol, but never of love. We must not let this come between us, Emily. Then, more than ever, I shall need your support, your understanding."

"I'll try," she promised, but the thought would not leave her. My baby will be born, and within a week, he will be another woman's husband. *I* must be sympathetic, but who will support and understand *me* when I shall be in my time of greatest need? The knowledge of this pain and degradation to come permeated her consciousness, it hung in the air like a miasma whenever they were together, and threatened to spoil the short time they had left to be all in all to one another.

"What kind of a marriage is this, for you to fear it so?" Simone tried to console her. "Is it the end of the world if he has to spend a few nights with her, now and then? Once she has born him a legitimate son, and heir to the throne, he may safely discard her."

Emily gave a bitter smile.

"It is easy for you to say, since you are not in love with him. For me, this argument is not so facile. My reason may accept that you are right, but my emotions are not persuaded."

"Then you must persuade them," Simone said, "since there is no other course open to you." The shrug of her shoulders was casual, but the message in her eyes was urgent – Emily must not falter now, for her own sake, and the sake of all those who had hitched their wagons to her star. "Think about your child, if you will not take heed for yourself," she went on. "In the event that the Princess has no offspring, he may one day sit upon the throne of Bilkhondar."

Emily looked up, with swift apprehension. "Surely that is not possible?" she queried.

"It has been known, I believe. If you are prepared to intrigue on his behalf . . ."

Emily shuddered. "I would rather have him strong and happy and well-educated," she said. For the first time since her confrontation with Prince Murad, she forgot her own plight, and began to wonder just what place her child would find in this feudal principality. The fog of discontent and self-pity lifted, and once again, her mind was actively occupied with more than her own problems. When the Prince arrived, she was full of nervous energy, eager to discuss the matter with him.

"Do not worry about him, he shall have the best of everything," Dara assured her. He always referred to the baby as "he", convinced from the first that it would be a boy. "We shall send him to England to be educated, and he will come back to take his part in the development of this country. I have told you – Bilkhondar will be very different in my reign."

His cheerfulness and confidence infected her, and she turned to him, smiling as he had not seen her smile for days.

"My brave Emily is back again, from wherever she has been," he said happily. "And not before time, as I have good news for her."

"What? What is it?" she clamoured to know.

"My father has agreed that we may obtain a doctor for you. I have been making enquiries for some time, and have learned of a Portuguese doctor living several days' journey away, on the coast. An English physician, even if one were available, would not be tolerated by my father. He will not have the British in his domain, since he distrusts them, and suspects them of seeking a foothold with the aim of annexing his territory in the end."

"A doctor is a doctor," Emily said delightedly. "So long as he is properly qualified, I am not particular as to his nationality."

"His qualifications are genuine, and he has a good reputation for his work. Apparently he lives with a local native woman, has many children, and is estranged from his fellow-Europeans. He is also chronically short of money, and therefore will be sure to come, since he will be well paid."

"Maybe you can persuade him to stay on, and he could be the start of your medical services," she said enthusiastically.

"Hm. If my father would allow it. It is a tremendous concession on his part to let this man enter the country. To permit him to enter the harem and assist at a birth, is hitherto unheard of."

"Yes," Emily agreed, "but then, it is a part of your bargain that my child is safely born, a prerequisite to the marriage he so much desires."

Prince Dara laughed with genuine amusement. "Life in Bilkhondar has made you cynical, my love. You will not allow my father a generous impulse?"

"I will not concede that any of his actions are motivated by concern for my welfare," she retorted drily.

"So long as you concede that mine are," he said, smiling, his eyes suddenly tender. "Come here – I have something else for you, besides news."

He opened his hand, and she saw that it held a silver ring such as the harem ladies often wore on their thumbs, a tiny mirror, mounted on a circlet of pearls. As she picked it up, he handed her a magnifying glass. "You will need this," he said.

Curiously, she turned the ring over, and saw that a line of minute lettering had been engraved on the back. "I had this done especially for you," he said. "Now let me see how good your command of Persian is."

Emily had no doubts on that score, since she had found herself fluent enough to dispute in that tongue with Prince Murad. She peered closely at the ring.

" 'Gar Firdaus bar rue zamin ast, Hamin ast, wa Hamin ast,' " she read carefully. " 'If there be paradise on earth, it is this, it is this, it is this.' Is that correct?"

"Perfect," he assured her. "They are the identical words to those Shah Jehan had written on the walls of his hall of Private Audience, but I think they apply just as well to us, to the love we share."

For a moment, she was so overcome by happiness that she could not speak. She had been heaped with jewellery more valuable, but this was precious to her because of the inscription, and the thought behind it.

She slipped it on to her thumb. "I shall wear it always," she said.

As the summer approached, Emily began to put on

weight, and found herself becoming breathless very easily, although otherwise fit and well. The climate of Bilkhondar, high in the Ghats, was generally benign, and did not suffer from the sweltering hot summers of the plains. All the same, by May it had begun to get quite hot, and she found it rather an effort to get around.

It was at this time, too, as the weather grew steadily hotter, that disturbing rumours began to filter in from the outside world. Forbidden though the women were to leave the harem, there were others, eunuchs, those who delivered the necessities of life, who touched both worlds, and through them news was brought of what was happening beyond the marble grilles, the palace walls, even beyond Bilkhondar itself. Qadir Bibi Bano, too, had sources of information she never divulged, but which were remarkably accurate.

"Strange things are happening in India, where the British rule," she said to Emily one day. "Word is being passed around that the British have mixed ground bullocks' bones with the flour."

Emily, who knew very well that to the largely Hindu population, such use of the sacred animal would be anathema, frowned slightly.

"I can't think why they should take such action, knowing it would incite the populace," she said. "It can't be true."

Qadir Bibi Bano shrugged. "True or not, what matters is that people believe it," she pointed out, reasonably enough. "They are saying, also, that Englishwomen are being brought to India to marry Indian princes, their children subsequently to be baptised as Christians. It is as well they do not know what is happening here, or it might add substance to the rumour."

Emily looked up sharply. "I am not married to

Prince Dara, nor likely to be," she said with acerbity, "and no mention has been made by me of baptising my child in any faith."

"You do not feel strongly about this matter of religion?" Qadir Bibi Bano queried gently.

"Not strongly enough to jeopardise a child's life, or his future," she said firmly. "My father always said I was a free-thinker. So if any such rumours are circulating here, you may squash them forthwith. What else is happening in India?"

"Oh . . . whisperings in the bazaars, cabbalistic signs being written on walls. Some say that chapattis – you know, the flat cakes of flour – are being passed from village to village as a way of circulating secret messages. There is much dissatisfaction among the people, and particularly among the native regiments."

Emily remembered suddenly a shipboard conversation overheard between her father and a major returning from leave. The major had bemoaned the fact that there was a general degeneration in the quality of British officers. Men were serving in India who had been unable to obtain commissions in England. Many of them were idle and slapdash, unable to stand the heat, over-dependent on huge retinues of servants. Some mistreated the men under their command, many more were simply unable to inspire respect. Her father had commiserated with his complaints, and agreed that the same lowering of standards was true of the employees of the East India Company.

She had worried about this at the time, and fully intended asking her father to expound further on the subject, but the opportunity had not arisen, the next day the storm had begun, and the incident had gone from her mind until this moment.

A day or two later, Simone was full of a horrific story

she had picked up in the harem corridors, about a young Indian sepoy by the name of Mangal Pande. It had happened back in March, but had taken some time to percolate through to Bilkhondar, via the bazaars and alleyways and villages.

Affected by the heat, and believing the British were about to murder the native soldiers, Mangal Pande had apparently gone berserk, and fired at the British adjutant and sergeant. His comrades did not join him, as he called on them to do, but neither did they attempt to disarm him. That task was left to an old soldier, General Hearsay, who alone had regained control of the situation.

"And what happened to Mangal Pande?" Emily asked.

"He was hanged, of course," Simone said. "Your compatriots must appear to have the upper hand, or all hell could break loose."

"How horrible," said Emily, shuddering with distaste at the mere thought of all this violence and bloodshed in the dominions she had once expected to find calm and at peace. "Are these isolated incidents, or is there going to be more unrest, I wonder?"

As usual when anything was troubling her, she discussed it with Prince Dara.

He said, "This is nothing new in itself, you know. As long ago as 1806, I believe, there was trouble in Vellore because of a new head-dress with a cockade believed to be fashioned from either cowhide or pigskin. The sepoys feared they were going to be forced to become Christians; they rose up during the night and murdered their officers in their beds. Then, more recently, there was a native regiment which refused to go to Burma because to cross the black waters meant pollution to orthodox Hindus. But you are right in believing that these occurrences are on the increase. It could mean serious trouble – an uprising, even, in India."

"But it need not touch us here, need it?" she asked, her thoughts at the moment concentrated on the coming child.

He frowned. "It need not . . . but that isn't to say it *will* not. I know my father has received secret emissaries from influential people who are considered dangerous in India, such as the Maulavi of Faizabad, the Rani of Jhansi, and the one they call the Nana Sahib, the Rajah of Bithur. I am not in his confidence regarding these messengers, indeed, I am not supposed to know of their visits."

"Do you think your father is involved in some kind of plot?"

"I think it would be premature to call it a plot. As yet, I believe, it is simply a matter of discussions between a number of discontented men who wish to turn an explosive situation to their advantage. But Emily, India is ripe for change, and if those who could bring about change peacefully, who could redistribute wealth and status and opportunity, won't do it, then the change will be violent. It is a hundred years since Clive won the battle of Plassey and laid the foundations of British power in India, and there is an old prophecy which states that this year, 1857, is the year in which that power will begin to crumble."

She sighed. "Oh, Dara – I wish it would all blow over. If it has to come sometime, then it has to, but not now!"

He gave a short, rather aggrieved laugh. "If I could, I would hold all India still until our child was born. But I am powerless even to influence what happens here in Bilkhondar. My father will not tell me what he is planning, which fact alone causes me to fear the worst. He is hiding his schemes from me because he knows I will not approve. I have had to employ subterfuge to discover what little I have already learned."

Emily paced restlessly up and down the room, then she stopped and turned to face him again.

"The latest news Qadir Bibi Bano has from India is something about rifles, but I did not understand it very well, nor, I think, did she."

"Possibly not. She is a clever woman, but without a great knowledge of ballistics, I should think. But the essentials of the argument are simple enough, if one does not get too technical."

The British authorities, he told her, had decided to replace the old "Brown Bess" smooth-bore musket currently in use, with the new Enfield rifle which had proved more effective. To load this new rifle, it was necessary to extract from a pouch a cartridge with a greased patch at the top, which had to be torn off with the teeth, and then used to ram the bullet down the barrel. The sepoys believed that the grease used was made from either pig fat or cow fat – one an abomination for Muslims, the other for Hindus.

"Apparently," said Dara, "this story began to be spread around after a low-caste worker at Dum Dum, near Calcutta, requested a drink from the bowl of a Brahmin sepoy. The sepoy refused on the grounds that the contact would defile him, and the man retorted that he need not be so fussy, since the cartridge grease would, anyhow, break his caste. Since then, there has been no stopping this rumour, and many sepoys are refusing to use the cartridges."

"And is the British government doing nothing to check it?" Emily asked.

"George Anson, the Commander-in-Chief of the army, ordered that the cartridges should be issued ungreased, but it was too late, Emily. Anyhow, he was overruled by the Governor-General, Lord Canning, who has decided, in his wisdom, to stand firm on the matter."

Emily shook her head. "It is bound to provoke trouble."

"It already has. Eighty-five sepoys at Meerut have been court-martialled for refusing the cartridge. They are almost certain to be found guilty. What the outcome of such a judgment will be, I dread to think."

Emily did the only thing she could. She tried not to think too much about it, and in this she was aided by nature. She had a little under two months to wait for the birth of her child, and in the way of women in her condition, the world had narrowed down, closed in, until it consisted of herself, her own body, and the strange, unknown other identity which had taken her over. When events in her world intruded, she pushed them away as far as she could, and hoped that whatever was going to happen would hang fire until she was once again herself and more able to face it.

But it was not to be. The world the British had created for themselves in India was about to dissolve in bloodshed and chaos, and afterwards, it would never again be quite as it was before. And the strange life of Emily Hunter was on the verge of yet another tempestuous upheaval.

That night, when it all began, towards the end of May, Dara had left her early, seeing that she was tired.

"Try to rest," he advised, and she settled down on the divan and closed her eyes, but for a long time, tired as she was, sleep eluded her, and she lay listening to the murmur of the fountains.

It seemed she had only just drifted off into a light sleep when she was roused by a commotion of voices and footsteps in the harem. Dimly, she was aware of a thudding sound, which, after a few moments' thought, she was able to identify as horses' hooves, many of them, beating across the main courtyard, where durbar was always held.

There was a light but urgent rapping on her door. "Enter," she called, and Simone burst agitatedly in.

"What's happening?" Emily asked her, pulling herself into a half-sitting position.

Simone's eyes were alight with her irresistible enjoyment of any drama.

"Something very exciting," she said. "Prince Murad's nobles have just ridden out with all their retainers, fully armed, with Prince Murad himself at their head."

Emily was on her feet now, her breath coming quickly.

"The harem is alive with rumours," the French girl continued. "It is said that the native sepoys have risen against the British in India. Politics I have never understood, and I don't see now why it should involve us here, in Bilkhondar, except that men can never resist a war, wherever it is."

At this juncture, they were joined by Qadir Bibi Bano, whose always impassive face was graver than ever.

"It is true, the sepoys have mutinied," she said, in reply to Emily's questioning gaze. "The whole of northern India is in ferment. And you –" she turned on Simone – "you are a fool if you think Bilkhondar can remain aloof from this. Like many of the Indian princes, Prince Murad sees in this uprising a chance to sweep the British into the sea. A messenger from his friend, the Nana Sahib of Bithur, was in the palace today."

The three women looked at each other silently, alarm and fear chasing the excitement from Simone's pert features as it dawned on her just how dangerous this could become.

Then there were footsteps in the corridor once more, and these were footsteps Emily knew, although she had seldom heard them in such haste. The door opened, and Dara stood there in his riding clothes, with a jewelled knife in his belt. Qadir Bibi Bano took one look at his grimly set face, and propelled the reluctant Simone towards the door.

He closed the door behind the two women, and crossed the room to Emily's side. Taking both her hands in his, he made her sit down on the divan, and sat down beside her.

"You must listen very attentively to what I am going to tell you, Emily," he said quietly. "I have only minutes, but I could not leave without seeing you, without telling you what is happening."

"Leave?" she said fearfully. "But where are you going?"

He put a finger to her lips to still her protests.

"You remember my telling you about the sepoys at Meerut who were court-martialled for refusing the cartridges for the new rifle?" She nodded, and he went on, "They were found guilty and sentenced to many years' hard labour, and publicly put in irons. The following day, May 10th, the native regiment rose in rebellion. There was terrible violence, Emily, such as I would hesitate to describe to you, were it not necessary for you to understand. Europeans murdered *en masse*, women, children. . . ."

She put a hand to her eyes as if to shut out the horror from her imagination; then, controlling herself, she said, "I'm better. Go on."

He said, "This rebellion is spreading across the northern part of India. The mutineers have taken Delhi, and you can envisage the slaughter there, in so important and populous a city. And they have found a rallying point – Mohammed Bahadur Shah, the last descendant of the Mogul dynasty."

"A Mogul king in Delhi – I did not know there was one," Emily said, surprised.

Dara gave a snort of mingled contempt and pity. "A poor, sick old man, living on a stipend from the East India Company. They say his mind wanders, and he lives in a filthy court, surrounded by debauched relatives. It is doubtful if he will find the mutineers less frightening than the British. Nonetheless, he is a Mogul Emperor's descendant, and it is enough for my father, who has thrown in his lot with the uprising. He sees it as a resurgence of the Mogul Empire."

"And how do you see it?" she challenged. He gave her a look of sober resignation. "As a military rebellion, not particularly well organized, which the British will put down, at whatever cost to themselves and others. You heard the horses ride out?"

She nodded, mute with apprehension.

"They are on their way to attack the British garrison down on the plain. As the crow flies, it is about thirty miles away, although through difficult, mountainous terrain. But the point is that my father has made no secret of his affiliation with the mutineers, and although he won't listen to me, and I can't convince him of it, the British are going to be waiting for him."

"Qadir Bibi Bano says other princes are joining the uprising."

"Yes, but they are all in northern India, far away from us. Between Bilkhondar and the areas where the mutiny has spread, lie hundreds of miles of safe

British-held territory, almost untouched by the trouble. My father believes others will rise with him. I doubt it. He believes he can annihilate this British garrison and set southern India alight, but they have sophisticated weapons, artillery, and his men have only their swords and antiquated muskets. It is suicide, Emily, and not only for him. When the British get here, a lot of innocent people are going to suffer in reprisals, whilst feelings are running high, as is already happening in India. We can't have this trouble in Bilkhondar, Emily. I have to stop it."

"You? How can you stop it?" she demanded agitatedly. "You are only one man. What are you planning to do?"

He gave a self-deprecating smile.

"To call it a plan is putting it rather strongly," he said. "I have gathered together a handful of the omrahs whom I have persuaded of the rightness of my course of action, and somehow, we must place ourselves between the opposing forces. I must go now, Emily. I have already lost too much time, and speed is essential if I am to hope for success. It is fortunate that I know the hills around Bilkhondar better than most, and we shall be able to travel swifter than my father's forces."

She seized his arm and clung to him tightly, terrified.

"No, Dara! You must not do it! It is dangerous to the point of foolhardiness!" she cried.

"Someone must stop this madness, and the responsibility has to be mine," he said gently. "I think you exaggerate the danger. I intend to act only as an intermediary. I shall not even be armed. See."

He drew the jewelled dagger from his belt, and tossed it carelessly down on the priceless Persian rug. "Is that not a symbol of my good faith?"

Emily was unconvinced.

"You may not be armed, but others will. Dara, please! Think of me! Think of the child!" she begged.

"Emily!" His voice was commanding now, almost strict, as she had never heard it before. "I, too, am the descendant of a Mogul Emperor, and so is the child you are carrying. Let us remember who we are, and act accordingly."

"*You* can remember who you are. I am only a woman who loves you."

"You are a subject of Queen Victoria, and you will grit your teeth and endure it, as thousands of your compatriots are having to do, all over India," he said, not without irony. His gaze softened again. "Truly, I think of little else but you and the child, but for now, I must think of Bilkhondar."

He pulled her to him, embraced her swiftly, and then he was gone. She ran from her apartments and down the corridor, regardless of her condition, and reached the marble grille overlooking the courtyard in time to see him mount Mr. Scrooge and ride out.

All that night she paced up and down the marble floor of her room, the child protesting violently within her.

"Emily, you must be calm," Simone exhorted her. "It is bad for you to upset yourself this way. You must rest."

It was in vain. She tried, but could not. Sleep was out of the question, and to remain still for more than a minute required superhuman self-control. For the first time, her spacious, beautiful rooms seemed to confine her, and if she ventured out into the other quarters of the harem, she could not escape the pitying attentions of the other women, none of whom were sleeping, in this, their country's crisis. Every few minutes she sent Simone to see if any news had filtered through, and the girl would come back with the information that there was none.

Towards dawn, she went out into the garden. The sky was rose, vermilion and silver, lightening to palest blue. A stupendous sunrise, promising another perfect, brilliantly hot day, but pleasant now, before the sun was fully awake. The fragrance of the roses was overwhelming, the fountain played its melodious, comforting music.

She breathed deeply, inhaling the peace of the quiet garden. Calm. Yes, she must be calm, even though she was in a tumult of fear and suspense. Forgive me, baby, she said, this night has been hard on you. I *will* lie down now, and let you rest.

Then she heard it, faintly in the distance at first, and coming steadily, inexorably closer. Drumbeats, and the massed footsteps and hoofbeats of an army on the move. Rhythmic, disciplined, a European army. And even as she listened, the discipline broke up, vanished in a welter of shooting, screaming and clashing, rising up towards them on the still, hot air from the city clustered at the feet of the palace.

There was a dull, ominous thud, and the very floor under her feet began to shake. Simone burst in without even a peremptory knock, and ran to join Emily in the garden. Her face was suffused with colour.

"*Ma foi!* The British are attacking the city of Bilkhondar!" she exclaimed. "And something is causing a stir in the courtyard. Come and see!"

The women of the harem were all pressed up against the marble grillework, gazing down in fear, consternation and excitement, and from here, the terrible sounds of the beleaguered city reached Emily's ears most clearly. Her countrymen were down there, and they were responsible for those sounds, for the mayhem tha was causing them, the screams of the wounded and dying, the ceaseless crack of rifle shots, the pounding of shells. Once, the thought of them so near would have filled her with joy – her rescuers. Now she turned away, sick at heart.

Pulling herself together, she looked for Qadir Bibi Bano. Within or without the harem, little happened without this influential woman's sources of information reporting it to her. Emily did not have to look far; the stout woman was at her elbow, steadying her youthful protégée with the force of her powerful personality.

"Courage, Excellent One," she said, unsmiling. "You, at any rate, have nothing to fear from them."

"Why are they here?" she asked, in her heart already knowing the answer.

"Prince Murad lost the battle and was killed in action," Qadir Bibi Bano said tersely. "And now your compatriots are slaughtering helpless women and children in the streets of the city."

Emily's grip tightened on the other woman's arm. "Oh, my God – it's too dreadful!" she said. "I can't believe it's true."

"It is true. You have only to listen."

"And Prince Dara – where is he?"

Qadir Bibi Bano did not answer, but stood grim and silent as a high-pitched, wailing lament began to spread amongst the women, one after another taking it up, until the zenana was filled with its eerie chorus. The older woman took Emily's arm and tried to draw her away from the grille, but the eyes of the women were riveted on something down there, something which was causing their uninhibited grief, and following their gaze, she saw what it was.

The huge main gates had been opened a little, just sufficiently to admit a dazed-looking peasant, in bloodstained clothing, leading in a riderless horse. As the gates were heaved shut behind them, Emily saw that the animal with the distinctive white blaze above its nose was Prince Dara's horse, Mr. Scrooge.

Emily screamed; instantaneously, a red-hot shaft of agony shot from right to left across her stomach. But for the strong, supporting arms of Qadir Bibi Bano, she would have collapsed as another spasm followed hard on the first. Inside her, there was a twisted sensation, as if the child was in a position that was causing it pain, from which it could not escape.

"Stop this uproar!" Qadir Bibi Bano rapped at the wailing women. "We have more to do than stand weeping. This child will be born before the day is over!"

"But there is more than six weeks to wait," Emily protested, in her ignorance of such matters. "The doctor is not here."

"Nonetheless." The older woman smiled a little. "You have suffered enough today to bring on the birth, and born it will be."

Emily was to remember little of that morning, beyond the pain, the pain and the sense of struggling futilely. It seemed to go on forever, while the sun rose high in the sky, and from the city below, the noise of the fighting, plundering and killing swelled into a crescendo of terror. She sweated and shrieked in the grip of an agony she had never realised could exist. In the midst of the pain and the bustle of activity all around her, only the presence of Qadir Bibi Bano was a constant calm, her cool hand on Emily's forehead, and her quiet, encouraging voice.

When finally the pain ceased, she could only lie there, at first conscious of nothing beyond relief that her body was no longer being torn apart. Then, slowly, it began to dawn on her that something was very wrong

She had given birth to a baby; babies cried. This one had not. She turned her head, and met the sympathetic eyes of Simone, who was at her side.

"Where is my baby?" she whispered with difficulty, for it was an effort even to speak.

Simone bent her head.

"It is dead, *chérie*," she said. "*Le pauvre petit*, it was dead at birth. It was much too early, and no doctor. You must not grieve too much."

Le pauvre petit. "A boy," Emily said. "A son. Where is my son? I want to see him."

"Hush, you will only upset yourself!" Simone said comfortingly. "The child will be buried quickly, as is the custom here, and it is better you do not see it."

Weak though she was, Emily's spirit had not entirely left her. She raised her parched voice.

"No! They shall not bury my baby before I have seen him! I must see him. Surely I have that right?"

Qadar Bibi Bano made her dignified way through the women surrounding the bed, and in her arms she carried a still, white bundle.

"It is well," she said to Simone. "Let her see him if she wishes."

Emily was raised slightly on her pillows, and the bundle was placed in her arms. He was the smallest baby she had ever seen, tightly wrapped in a white shroud which covered all but his tiny face. Though hopelessly premature, the small, pinched features were perfectly formed, Dara's fine Persian nose and almond-shaped eyes, a tuft of pale brown hair showing beneath the shroud. Emily held him for a moment, then handed him back to Qadir Bibi Bano. She did not cry. She wished that she could, but this was an anguish that could not find easy relief in tears.

Meeting the older woman's eyes, she said, without

apparent emotion, "Prince Dara is dead, too. Isn't he?"

Steadfastly, she gazed back. "Yes," she said quietly. "He rode between Prince Murad and the British, and was shot down."

It was as if she had always known that it would happen. He had tried to prevent the confrontation between his father and the British, but the latter had mistaken or disregarded his intentions. Someone had fired unthinkingly, and ended the life of the one man who could, at some future date, have eased their path into Bilkhondar in less tragic circumstances. Whoever had fired that shot had also put out the light of her life. There was nothing left.

Qadir Bibi Bano held a silver cup to Emily's lips, with something unpleasant-tasting in it. She swallowed it obediently, uncaring. It might as well have been poison.

"Sleep now," the woman said. "This will help you." Emily rolled over and succumbed to exhaustion.

CHAPTER
SEVEN

WHEN she awoke again, it was night, although not the soft, lamplit night of the harem, to which she had grown accustomed. Something was obviously wrong, and she lay there, slowly regaining her senses and trying to work out what it was.

In her apartment, where as many as half a dozen lamps usually glowed, only one feeble night-light flickered; the beautiful room was deep with shadows. No moonlight shone in from the garden, only an eerie red glow, pulsating through a pall of smoke and dust. An acrid smell filled the air, and the splashing of the fountains was drowned by the guns which now were ominously near.

Still weak from the day's ordeal, Emily turned her head listlessly, too indifferent to her fate to rise from her bed. Let them come, let them burn down the palace if they wished. She sighed heavily, and then perceived that she was not alone; Simone crouched at her bedside.

"Emilie? You are awake?" The French girl's voice was hoarse with fear, any glamour possessed by the invading army had long since given way to terror.

"Yes."

"The British are attacking the palace. It has been going on for hours, all the time you were asleep, drugged. The guards left by Prince Murad are fighting to the death, but they are losing, inch by inch."

"Then why do they bother?" Emily said wearily, distantly. "Who do they not simply surrender, since in the end, it is inevitable they will be overcome? Prince Murad is dead. Prince Dara is dead. There is nothing left to defend."

"*Mon dieu!*" cried Simone, almost in tears. "You have lost your man and your child in twenty-four hours, I know, but I think you have also lost your reason! They fight because the alternative is not to be considered. Bilkhondar is now a rebel state, and the British are giving no quarter to rebels."

"A flag of truce," Emily suggested indifferently, as though none of it had anything to do with her. "That would surely not be violated."

"They are not interested in a truce. No prisoners are being taken," Simone stated flatly. "And the guards are not only defending themselves, but defending us, also, inside the harem." She touched the silken edge of her sari. "Do not think these will save us," she said, distraught.

"British soldiers will not harm women," Emily said, but doubtfully, her mind beginning to emerge from the mists of the sleeping draught she had been given.

"Will they not? Mutineers have butchered women and children, and the British army is responding in like manner. It is happening, *chérie*, in India, it has happened in Bilkhondar, this very day. The only hope you and I have is that our white skins will save us, but in the heat of the moment . . ." she shuddered.

"They can have my skin with the greatest of pleasure," Emily said, turning her face to the wall again. "I have no further use for it."

"Well, I have plenty of uses for mine!" Simone retorted vehemently. "I am only twenty-five, and I do not want to die!"

Emily gazed into the flickering blue flame of the small lamp. Oh Dara, she thought, your son was born today, and I saw him, held him for a few moments, before he was taken from me for ever, as you have been. Now it has all gone, all our dreams, and I must say goodbye to you. But I can't. Only death can release me.

The room, the smoke-filled gardens beyond, the entire palace, and the reddened night sky, shook in a final, tremendous onslaught of cannon fire. There were running feet, heavy and booted, many of them, hoarse, male voices shouting with a kind of obscene triumph. Inhuman yelps and cries rent the corridors outside, and screams, the screams of terrified women.

Simone gripped Emily's hands so tightly that her nails drew blood.

"They are here – in the harem!" she gasped. "The guards, the eunuchs on the inner doors, even – all must be dead! What are we going to do?"

Even as she spoke, the door burst open, and the two slave-girls, Gulal and Yasmin, burst in, almost incoherent with fright as they flung themselves on the floor at Emily's side.

The last of the mists cleared, and Emily's mind was her own again, free and reasoning and fully aware of the danger. Even now, it did not matter to her if she were alive or not, her instincts of self-preservation were gone, and her desire was for oblivion. But something else did matter, a real affection for these people with whom she had spent the best part of a year, who had cared for her, and linked their lives and their interests with hers. She could not lie here and leave them to their fate.

"Hush," she said comfortingly to the distraught girls, and then another thought came to her. "Where is Qadir Bibi Bano? I have not seen her."

Simone pointed wordlessly to the door. Of course. Where else would the fat woman be in a crisis, but in the centre of it, doing whatever she could for the girls in her charge? As she had always done for Emily herself, however much they might have misunderstood one another at the start.

Emily slid her feet to the floor and stood up. She was momentarily dizzy, for it was only a few hours since she had suffered a complicated and protracted labour. She steadied herself, breathing deeply, and walked swiftly out into the main halls of the harem, into a scene she would never forget.

Here, too, only the faint night-lights burned, and in the shadows, groups of frightened women huddled together, sobbing hysterically. The scarlet coats of the soldiers were everywhere, and every man had a bayonet fixed to his rifle. Some were intent on plunder, and were careless in their eagerness to loot, smashing priceless vases and tearing rich fabrics as they grabbed whatever they could hold. Others clearly had different but equally dangerous intentions; one man had seized one of the girls by the arm, and was dragging her across the floor. She shrieked wildly, and struggled in vain. All of the British wore the same grim, vengeful, murderous expressions on their faces, and the officers in charge were doing nothing to restrain their excesses.

Transfixed and half-hidden by one of the pillars, Emily watched as a bloody little scene was enacted not twenty feet away from her. Quadir Bibi Bano, like a battleship in full sail, bore down on the soldier who was manhandling the girl. She pulled the sobbing girl from his grasp, thrust her away, and harangued the man in rich, scornful Persian phrases, referring contemptuously to his parentage, and his obvious baseness in maltreating a helpless woman. He looked at her coldly his face set and unmoved, and in one swift, clean action, drove his bayonet between her ribs.

Qadir Bibi Bano emitted one gasp of mingled pain and incredulity, swayed and fell heavily to the ground. She clutched herself, moaned and then lay still, blood making an obscene pool on the white marble floor.

Now that the first blood had been spilled in the harem, the first woman killed, it seemed a Rubicon had been crossed. Bayonets fixed, the men advanced, slowly and inexorably, their looting abandoned. There were greater spoils here. There was vengeance for the women of Delhi and Meerut, for the besieged garrison of Cawnpore and the Residency of Lucknow, whose sufferings had just begun. And there was a simple, elemental bloodlust, known to men in time of war throughout the ages. The women screamed and retreated, and the men advanced.

Emily came to life. In all her remaining years, she was never to know if she could have taken such action if her own life had held any meaning, any future, and in her maturity, she doubted it, and refused to claim any heroism in what she did. Mainly it was pity and revulsion and indignation, and a scathing disregard for her own worth. She ran forward, placing herself between the soldiers and the women, holding out her hands in a gesture that forbade them to advance any further.

"Stop!" she shouted, clearly, loudly, and in English. "For God's sake, stop this madness!"

Her words, spoken in their own language, shrilled into their mass consciousness, but alone, they might not have sufficed. What arrested them was something she had genuinely forgotten, since it was so long since she had seen herself as she appeared to a European male

– her red-blonde hair, streaming loose and dishevelled over her shoulders, the angry, blue-grey eyes, and the translucently pale skin.

As one man, they came to a halt, and their threatening attitude melted into amazement. They stared at her, and she stared back at them, all fear gone, now, the situation defused. These were once more men she could handle.

"Who is in charge here?" she demanded.

"I am, ma'am." He could not have been more than twenty-eight, and looked younger, yet he had a hard, calculating face. "George Hargreaves, major, 1st Deccan Rifles, at your service."

He looked down at her, not from a great height, as he was not tall, but he made it seem an act of condescension, in spite of the cold civility of his address. Emily thought, I must watch this one, we are not quite out of the woods yet.

"Then, Major Hargreaves, would you mind asking your men to take those . . . those *things* off their rifles? I find it difficult to converse sensibly with all that cold steel pointed at me."

"Unfix bayonets, men. We are frightening the lady," drawled the Major. Someone laughed, and he turned sharply and repeated the order, which was instantly obeyed. Emily saw that whatever had happened in the city, and here in the palace, had taken place with the full cognisance of this officer; he was perfectly capable of controlling his men if he chose to. He turned his attention once more to Emily.

"You have the advantage of me, ma'am."

"I do beg your pardon. I am Emily Hunter. *Miss* Emily Hunter," she emphasised.

The Major gave her a stiff, formal little bow, she responded with a curt nod of her head.

"Now we have introduced ourselves, might I point out to you that one of your men has just murdered a woman?" she said frostily, shivering inwardly with rage and grief, but holding herself taut.

"Miss Hunter," the Major replied patiently, as if explaining something to an idiot or a small child, "might I point out to *you* that I and my men have just captured a rebel state. This was not accomplished without a certain amount of bloodshed."

"I am aware that men kill each other in battle. I was not aware that your duties included killing women in cold blood."

"No, ma'am. We learned that from the mutineers at Delhi," sneered the Major.

"But Major, no British women have been killed in Bilkhondar. To the best of my knowledge, I am the sole representative of my country in this principality, and as you can see, I am alive and unharmed." As she spoke the last sentence, a wave of dizziness washed over her, and she held a hand briefly to her forehead. Regaining control, she went on, "The dead woman has never been outside the gates of the harem since her youth, she was innocent of anything other than trying to protect her companions from your men."

"It is regrettable," Major Hargreaves said stiffly, and more than that he would not concede.

Warning bells clanged in Emily's brain; she saw, she understood that the situation was once again becoming ugly. The Major obviously had no intention of subjecting the man responsible for Qadir Bibi Bano's death to any kind of punishment, and if she persisted in being stiff-necked, she would lose all she had gained for the women in the harem. She could do nothing, now, for Qadir Bibi Bano, and that person, always a realist, would not have wished her to jeopardise the lives of the girls she had sought to protect. Emily climbed down, as graciously as she could.

"As you say. Perhaps I could have your assurance that there will be no further incidents such as this?"

"Certainly, if I can have yours that there will be no acts of resistance. My men do not take kindly to knives in their backs, or poison in their food."

"There will be nothing of that kind, so long as the women are treated with respect," Emily affirmed boldly, since there was nothing else she could do but behave as if she could command such assurance. "If you will permit them to attend to the body of their friend. . . . Perhaps you will take tea in my apartments?"

"Tea?" the Major said, incredulously. "You mean – with milk and sugar?"

"Cream, if you like," Emily said coolly. "That is, unless you have reduced the kitchens to rubble."

"Ma'am," he said, his upper lip curling slightly, "have you not heard that the British army marches on its stomach? I never destroy kitchens, or cooks, if I can avoid it."

Loathing of this man who had commanded the action which killed Dara, brought on the premature birth of her child, slaughtered the citizens of Bilkhondar wholesale, and finally, caused the brutal murder of her dear friend, and the mainstay of the harem, rose in Emily's throat as she turned her back and preceded him to her apartments. She forced it down again, sensing a volatile and potentially violent personality, whose actions were not wholly predictable.

The major's eyes widened perceptibly at the opulence of Emily's quarters. She saw him taking in the Persian carpets, the silken hangings, the books and, with astonishment, the pianoforte. As he wandered around, eyeing and fingering, she summoned Simone and the slave-girls from where they crouched, still shivering, at the foot of the divan.

"Send down to the kitchens and order English tea, with the silver tray and the china service, as they used to serve it for Prince Dara," she said, speaking in French, as she always did when talking to Simone. "Then go to all parts of the harem and pass the word; the palace has formally surrendered, and no attacks of any kind are to be made on the lives of the British officers and men."

Simone was staring, half-afraid, half-fascinated, at the aforesaid British officer in his perambulations around the room, and Emily took her friend by the shoulders and shook her. "Go quickly. This man is not to be tried too far. They have killed Qadir Bibi Bano, and can only be trusted insofar as we can keep them pacified. Take this, if you want some kind of authority for my orders."

She wrenched off the silver ring Prince Dara had given her, which bore his initials beneath the inscription.

"Bring it back to me, if you can," she said, more gently, remembering she had promised to wear it always. "Go on." She gave Simone a slight push, as the French girl hesitated. "Do as I say, and all will be well. I have the Major's word."

Simone sped on her way, and turning to the slave-girls, Emily switched automatically into Marathi.

"Please light the lamps. It is rather gloomy in here." They would have left after performing this duty, but she ordered them to stay in the apartment, although unobtrusively. She had no wish to be alone with the hard-faced Major.

"You would appear to be a mistress of tongues," he said, curiously.

"Hardly. I can make myself understood. The girl I spoke to first is French, and naturally, I learned that language at home in England."

"Naturally," said the Major with heavy sarcasm, and she guessed he had not had the benefit of such education. "You live in some luxury too, I see. Your every whim catered for. Your orders obeyed unquestioningly. How do you come to hold a position of such eminence here, Miss Hunter?"

"I don't." Emily sensed that this man was nosing around uncomfortably near the truth, and she was not about to tell him the story of her love affair with Prince Dara. "But as you know, there is now no real authority within the harem, or within the palace – apart from that wielded by yourself."

She knew that he was not entirely convinced of her personal insignificance, but his curiosity had moved on elsewhere.

"In fact, if I may ask, what has been puzzling me since I first set eyes on you, is how you come to be here at all."

"I was shipwrecked on the way to Bombay with my father, who worked for the Company. I believe I was the sole survivor of the wreck. I was brought here unconscious, so I know little of how I arrived, and I have been here since last September. I have been kindly treated, and not harmed in any way," she added firmly, setting aside the twice-attempted murder, and the nightmare confrontation with Prince Murad.

"Oh come, Miss Hunter," said Major Hargreaves, his voice polite, but his eyes insolent. "Do you take me for a fool? This is a harem, is it not?"

It was anger, more than embarrassment, which caused Emily's face to flush to the hair-roots. He was fishing for salacious details of assaults upon her person, and he was not going to hear of any such thing from her. Not only because she disliked him instinctively, and would have died rather than discuss such matters with him, but because she was not going to give him anything he could twist and use as an excuse for reprisals against the girls in the harem. She saw that it would, anyhow, have been useless to tell him that she had lived happily, and of her own volition, as the Prince's favourite; such a man as this would be unlikely to believe her.

"I think, sir, you must have been reading too many of the novels of Ouida," she said lightly. "For most of the women here, most of the time, life is as circumscribed as that in a young ladies' academy. Only a very few find . . . favour, shall we say."

Fortunately, just then Simone arrived back with the tea, and Emily was never so glad to escape from a conversation, or to find an opportunity to sit down. She was tired beyond expression, both physically and in her mind, but this man must not know that only a few hours ago, she had borne and lost a child.

And so, as dawn broke once more over the battered city and the defeated palace, the women's quarters were quiet and subdued, and Emily Hunter sat in her apartment, drinking tea from china cups with the new commander.

For the next few days, Major Hargreaves kept his promise not to molest the women of the harem, although his men patrolled the corridors, and their presence was always felt. The women took to moving about everywhere veiled, except for Simone, who made a point of doing the opposite – no one was going to mistake *her* for a native woman, and slit her throat in an unfriendly moment, she told Emily.

As for Emily, the mantle of Qadir Bibi Bano seemed to have fallen on her shoulders, and every problem, every need, every worry, was brought to her ears. She found herself settling petty arguments, reassuring small fears, giving orders for practical necessities, as well as acting as unofficial liaison officer between the harem and the British. What time she had left, she spent resting in her room, conserving her slowly returning strength.

The Major made a point of visiting her every day, although she would gladly have forgone his company. On each occasion, he made it clear he expected tea to be served, and Emily complied with as good a grace as she could, since he held the safety of all of them in his hands, and his power of life or death was, in those first, uneasy days, as literal as Prince Murad's had been.

"Ugh – that man!" Simone said distastefully, clearing up the tea-things after his latest visit. "Perhaps we should introduce him to the Princess Jani, and if we are fortunate, she will poison him."

Emily raised her eyebrows. "Not if you value your own lives, for you need his goodwill, odious though it is to have to court it," she said. "Incidentally, how is Her Highness taking this new turn of events?"

Simone put the tray down on the table, and sat down herself. Emily had been silent and withdrawn, or cold and purposeful, since Dara's death; this was the first inclination she had shown to gossip or chat.

"Immured in her apartments, refusing to speak to anyone," she said. "It is said that now there is no chance of marriage for her, she wishes to return home to her father, but whom can she ask?"

"I shall speak to the Major about it," Emily said briskly. "Clearly, her father did not hold the frontier against the British, so they should not bear him or his daughter any ill-will. There is no reason why she should stay here."

Simone gaped at her.

"You would help to send her home? After what she tried to do to you? I was right – this thing has sent you half-crazed," she declared.

Emily's face was calm and expressionless. "How will it help me if she stays here against her will? Can it bring Dara back to life? No, it cannot, therefore it is of no consequence. I feel no enmity towards her. I feel nothing at all, Simone, can't you understand? Emotion is all gone. I am a void."

Simone picked up the tray again, sensing that she had been mistaken.

"You feel loyalty and friendship, *chérie*," she said gently, "or else you would not trouble yourself on our behalf. And you also experience displeasure when the major uses Prince Dara's china – I have seen it in your eyes. I do not believe you are dead yet."

Without waiting for Emily to contradict her, she swept out of the room.

The next day, they noticed a change in the habits of their new rulers. The men withdrew completely from the inner courts of the harem, and although they still patrolled the walls and guarded the outer gates, at least the women's once private quarters were free of their booted feet and staring eyes.

"What have you done?" Simone asked suspiciously. "What kind of persuasion have you used, to cause the Major to take his men out of the harem?"

Emily looked up, questioningly. "I am not responsible for this, I did not even have any prior knowledge of it. And how should I have influenced Major Hargreaves? He pays scant attention to my wishes."

"It is because of you that we are alive at all," Simone reminded her.

"If that is so, it is because I am an Englishwoman,

and he does not – quite – dare allow his men to commit unspeakable offences before my eyes," Emily said tartly. "Personally, our military gentleman does not like me at all."

"He may not like you, but he finds you interesting," Simone rejoined shrewdly. "I thought perhaps you had been – how should I say it – encouraging him?"

Emily shuddered.

"How could you even think it? Prince Dara has not been dead a week, and I am in no mood to flirt with a man I find offensive. I'm not sure I even know how to flirt. Not that it matters, since I shall never care for a man again."

"Never is a long time when one is nineteen," said Simone. "What will you do?"

Her friend's eyes were blank. "Do? What do I care? What does it matter?"

Simone said, "*Chérie*, it is right and natural that you should grieve. No one could have the love of a man like Prince Dara, and lose him without grieving. But you are like a sleep-walker. Since the moment you heard of his death, you have not shed a tear. Mourn him. All of us here understand and wish to support you in your loss. You must come to it sometime, and the later you come to it, the worse it will be for you."

When she was alone, Emily went out into the garden. Since the moment you heard of his death, you have not shed a tear. . . . Simone was right, she knew. She should have wept and torn at her hair, and smashed things, and they would all have rushed to comfort her. They thought her cold and strange because she had not.

But from that moment, when she saw the riderless horse led in, and realised what had happened, she had not been allowed a breathing space. She had been shocked into giving birth, then the palace was under attack, then there was the Major, and the necessity of protecting the girls. Her time for grieving had been denied her, she had been robbed of it, it had turned inward on her and frozen around her heart, like a stone in a petrifying well. And now, she thought, it was too late for the cathartic, healing tears of mourning. This sorrow was locked up inside her for the rest of her life.

The women of the harem could scarcely believe their good fortune in being left in comparative peace once more. Tentatively, they removed their veils and wandered around talking to each other more freely than they had done since the British invasion. Emily, too, was relieved that the day had brought no visit from the Major, but precisely at four o'clock, Simone bustled excitedly in with a note on a silver salver.

"There is a British officer at the main door, and he gave me this for you," she said.

"Another officer? I do not desire to speak to any of Major Hargreaves' lieutenants, or whatever," Emily said firmly.

"No, no, this is an older man, a senior officer, I am sure. Major Hargreaves was there too, and addressed him as 'sir'. He has a kind face," Simone said. "At least, read the note."

Emily unfolded the paper and read the short message, written in a neat, well-formed hand.

> Dear Miss Hunter,
>   Your presence here has only just been brought to my notice, and if it is convenient, I should like to pay my respects.
>   Your obedient servant,
>   Henry J. Smythe (Colonel)
>   1st Deccan Rifles

Emily gave a small, derisive laugh. "My obedient servant, indeed!" she said. "Well, in any event, he has a different style from that of the Major. *Billets-doux* on silver trays, no less! And he is a colonel, so we had better allow him to pay his respects. Oh, and don't forget the tea, Simone."

Simone shook her head forebodingly at the lightly veiled bitterness in her friend's voice, but she scurried off to escort the visitor through the harem, pausing only to dispatch Gulal for the tea.

He came alone, knocked on the door, and waited for her to call "Come in," before he entered. Emily, fearing the worst, owing to her recent experiences, and preparing herself for the kind of verbal combat she was accustomed to with the Major, saw a man of her father's age, grey-haired and with a deeply-furrowed brow. It was a stern, strong face, but she saw why Simone had called it kind, for the eyes were infinitely sympathetic. She knew that her fears were groundless.

"Miss Hunter." The Colonel bowed over her hand. "Forgive me for not giving you greater warning of my visit, but I was most anxious to reassure myself of your well-being."

"It is kind of you to be concerned, Colonel, but I am perfectly well," she replied.

There was a pause as Gulal brought the tea, and Emily indicated that the girl should leave. She felt quite safe alone with Colonel Smythe.

He said, "Are you by any chance related to Edward Hunter, who worked for the Company in Bombay?"

"I am his daughter! Did you know my father?"

"We were slightly acquainted. I remember meeting him at a dinner party in Bombay, oh, it must have been all of two years ago, and he had spoken of a daughter then, but I could not remember her name. I heard about the ship being lost, without survivors, and when Hargreaves told me of the circumstances of your coming here, it jogged my memory."

He accepted the cup of tea Emily poured for him, and noted the smile that lit her sad face as he mentioned her father.

"My dear girl," he said. "So you have been imprisoned here for almost a year? What a ghastly thing to have happened."

Her slight, impatient gesture swept away her own plight.

"I have long since ceased to consider it imprisonment. I am alive and unharmed, which is more than can be said for many of the erstwhile inhabitants of Bilkhondar. *You* should have been the one to take Bilkhondar. Oh, why couldn't it have been you?"

His eyes met hers over the rim of the teacup, his expression grim.

"I should, indeed," he said. "This is my regiment, and this was the most important action they have ever been involved in. And where was I, when Bilkhondar rose for the mutineers?" He set down his cup, disgustedly. "I was on leave in Poona. Major Hargreaves was the man on the spot, and it fell to him to deal with the situation. Are you suggesting I might have dealt differently with it?"

"Colonel Smythe," Emily said quietly, "are you implying that you might not?"

He hesitated, as if considering whether he should back his second-in-command to the hilt, then he abandoned the idea, and shook his head, sighing heavily.

"Very often it is necessary to hang or shoot guilty rebel ringleaders; in extreme circumstances it may be necessary to execute without proof of guilt, but if you are asking me if I agree with wholesale killing, I have to admit that I don't like it."

"Your second-in-command does. Have you ridden through Bilkhondar, Colonel? I hear it is not a pretty sight."

"Hargreaves is a capable enough officer, if somewhat over-conscientious about certain aspects of his profession. His orders were to take Bilkhondar and crush the rising. No limitations were imposed as to how he did it."

"The man is a sadist," Emily said. "Here, in the harem itself, a woman who was my friend was brutally murdered, before our eyes. Others would have been killed the same way, if my presence had not . . . had not been discovered. And if you are going to say that this was in reprisal for what happened at Delhi, I have heard that before, Colonel!"

Emily was trembling, now, with anger and retrospective shock, as she relived those awful moments. The Colonel placed his large, capable hands on her shoulders, and held her still.

"Listen to me, now, Emily. I am going to take the liberty of calling you Emily, since I am going to talk to you as if you were my own daughter. The first point is this; privately, I may agree with you, privately, I may indicate to Major Hargreaves my opinion of his handling of the situation. But with feelings running as high against the mutineers as they are at present, it would be impossible for me even to reprimand him publicly, let alone impose any punishment.

"The second point is this – you must put a guard on the sympathy you feel for these people."

"But why? Why should I not feel sympathy for them?" Emily interposed excitedly. "I have lived among them for almost a year, I have friends here. I am English, it is true, but in a sense, these are almost my own people."

"Your thoughts, your emotions, are your own, but you must at least modify your expression of them, for no one will share them with you," the Colonel said sternly. "You will meet with misunderstanding at best, more often with outright hostility, in India."

"I am not in India," she pointed out.

"Technically, you are in British India already," he reminded her. "Soon you will be there in actuality, for I propose sending you to Poona."

Emily jumped to her feet; the china teacup fell to the ground and smashed to pieces.

"No! I don't wish to leave here!" she declared forcefully.

The Colonel's face was puzzled.

"Don't you want to return home, eventually?"

"Home?" she repeated blankly. "Oh, you mean to England. No, I have no family there, no ties. All I want is to be left here, to live peacefully."

Had she not been so agitated at the prospect of being sent away, she could have found it in herself to feel sorry for him. He was kind and courteous, but he didn't understand. He came on a mission of rescue, to return a young English lady to her people and her proper station in life, and he found a half-crazed girl who wanted to spend the rest of her days immured in the zenana of a dead prince.

"My dear," he said gently, "you cannot stay here. It would be unseemly for you. For the present, Bilkhondar is under military rule, but if the surrounding Indian territory stays quiet, and we get the upper hand of this rebellion, we shall have the full paraphernalia of civilian government, officials and their wives. It would not be right for a young British lady to be living here in a harem."

"The memsahibs would not like it," said Emily.

"Indeed they would not. And to be truthful, I do not much like it myself. Let it go, Emily. What has happened to you in this past year is so incredible as to be unreal, a bizarre episode. Put it all behind you, take up the threads of your life where you left them."

She shook her head.

"No, I can't. This was real. So real that by comparison, everything else will be pale shadows. *This* was the reality. What follows is only the dream."

She saw that he was looking strangely at her, and knew that she must tell him what she had withheld from Major Hargreaves, the part of the story he had not heard.

"You are speaking to Miss Emily Hunter, but in truth, she no longer exists, and I cannot go back to her life," she explained. "The woman you see before you now is called Nadira. She was the favourite of Prince Dara, and on the day your forces took Bilkhondar, she gave birth to his stillborn child."

He stared at her, still only half believing. "Is this true?"

"I swear to you. Every word. So you see, I am not what you thought I was."

"It is not for me to pass judgment. You did what you had to do."

I did what I wanted to do, was on the tip of her tongue, but before she could say it, he looked questioningly at her, and asked, "Who, then, is the Prince Dara of whom you speak? The Prince who fell in the battle was Murad, surely?"

"Prince Dara was his son."

"Wait a minute. The one who was sent to England to

study? Very little information has come out of Bilkhondar, our intelligence people have found it virtually impossible to penetrate."

Emily buried her head in her hands. So it had all been for nothing, that mad, quixotic ride into the night to try to stop the tragedy. Someone had shot him down without even knowing whom they had killed, a pointless, meaningless death for a brave man who had been at odds with his time, who had sought to save others from suffering. And had failed. And not one iota of difference had it made. Hargreaves and his men had killed and burned and looted. Prince Murad had died, the city had fallen, and for what purpose had the man she loved given his life?

She had taken it all, endured it, and not wept, she had begun to accept his death, but she could not accept this, this futility. Something came adrift inside her, the ice loosened, and she began to cry, but there was nothing remedial in her tears, they were bitter and angry and hysterical.

The Colonel put his arms round her, and in the confusion of the moment, he was no longer a strange man she had met for the first time this afternoon, he was a rough, fatherly shoulder to rail against and cry on – he was her father. He could not help her, he could only dimly understand the cause of her wild grief, but he let himself be used, he held her and allowed her to cry until she was finished.

After a time, she gained a measure of control, and dried her eyes on the large handkerchief he offered her.

"Thank you. I'm sincerely sorry for my behaviour," she said. "I don't usually give way to attacks of self-pity."

"It would be quite understandable if you did," he said kindly, "after all you have gone through. Now, more than ever, I am convinced of the necessity of getting you away from here, as much for your own good as for the sake of appearances. No, don't argue, my dear. My mind is made up, and you know now that I have the authority to enforce any decisions I make."

Looking at his face, she saw that it would be pointless to plead, cajole, or stubbornly resist. Kind he might be, but underneath the amiability was a steely resolution, and as he had politely pointed out, he could send her away without her consent if he chose to do so.

"What more can I say?" She shrugged helplessly, and reflected fleetingly on the ignominy of being a woman, who could use her wits, her feminine wiles, to gain her ends, but ultimately was defenceless in the world of men. "But where do you intend sending me? I know no one in Poona."

"To my wife. Our own two girls are at school in England, and she will treat you as if you were our daughter. Do not worry too much about the future. Be content to let that take care of itself, and give yourself space to recover from your ordeal."

On the point of relinquishing responsibility for the harem, Emily remembered the Princess Jani.

"Will you do something for me, Colonel?"

"If I can."

"There is a young woman in the harem, a princess from a neighbouring state. She was to have been the bride of Prince Dara. I do not know her personally, but I have heard she wishes to return to her father."

"I will do what I can," he promised. "And you . . . how soon will you be fit to travel?"

She smiled faintly. "Oh, almost immediately. If I must go, there is no point in prolonging the farewells."

After the Colonel had gone, Simone came at once, agog to know what had taken place.

"So? What does he have to say, our new commander with the kind face and the smart uniform?"

"He says I am to be sent to Poona, to stay with his wife," Emily said, "and nothing I say or do will persuade him to let me stay here."

The French girl did not evince any great surprise.

"Well, no. With the British in charge, it would not be right. We had better pack. But what?" she frowned, pursed her lips thoughtfully. "Nothing we have is suitable for Poona. We have no European clothes."

Emily sat back, regarding her friend suspiciously.

"What is this 'we'?" she wanted to know.

"But of course. You must have a personal maid. The Colonel will not expect you to travel, or to live, without one."

"I thought you did not care for Poona very much."

"Poona is quite pleasant, especially in the hot weather. What I did not care for was that dreadful woman I worked for. With you it will be different – I can impose upon your good nature," Simone said cheerfully. Her face took on a more serious expression as she continued, "*Chérie*, we have been through too much together for me to let you go into the future alone. Prince Dara is gone, Qadir Bibi Bano is gone, and now you are leaving. There is nothing here for me, now. Do you not desire my company?"

Emily took the other girl's hand. "More than anything. With you, it will not seem so bad," she said with feeling.

CHAPTER
EIGHT

EVEN with Simone's support, it was bad enough, when the day came for them to leave Bilkhondar. Sadly Emily said goodbye to the women of the harem, who had seemed so alien at first, but were now her friends; to the two slave-girls, Gulal and Yasmin, who wept openly.

For the last time, she walked around her apartments remembering only the happy times, the ecstatic moments. For the last time, she stood in her beloved garden and listened to the fountains playing. She thought she would take their music with her, whereve she went.

The previous day, Emily and Simone had chosen horses from the palace stables for their journey. Simone, who was unused to riding, had chosen the quietest-looking mount. Emily had pointed to Mr Scrooge.

"I'll take that one," she had said.

"A mettlesome nag," agreed Major Hargreaves enviously. "Had my eyes on him myself."

Emily had stared levelly at him. Over my dead body, she thought, will you ride Prince Dara's horse, under no other circumstances. "The Colonel said we migh choose any horses we pleased, and I have decided o that one," she replied coolly.

Now the horses were saddled up and waiting in th courtyard.

"It is time, *chérie*," Simone said quietly. "Come – let us go now."

The harem doors closed behind them, once and for all. The woman called Nadira ceased to exist, and Emily Hunter rode reluctantly away from Bilkhondar, less than a year older, and changed utterly.

Emily, Simone, and the detachment of soldiers Colonel Smythe had allotted to escort them on their journey, arrived in Poona after dark, so as not to draw attention to the outlandish sight of two white women in native Indian dress. The Colonel's wife was waiting to greet them, with refreshments ready on hand, there was the welcome luxury of a hot bath, and clean, comfortable beds after the hard journey. There was blessedly little talk, for which Emily was thankful, and then there was the utter relief of sleep.

The famous hill station, to which officials and their families came seeking refuge from the heat of the plains during the hot weather, was an uneasy place during the summer of 1857. Though far south of the troubled area, no one knew, then, whether the uprising would be stamped out, or whether it would spread to engulf the entire sub-continent. There was a noticeable absence of men, particularly in uniform, since all available military personnel were being dispatched to the rebellious area. There was, even more noticeably, an atmosphere of distrust. Although life went on, outwardly, as normally as was possible, a gulf was widening day by day between the races. The British were looking askance at trusted servants who had worked for their families for years, and wondering if the hands that prepared meals and pulled punkahs would, in the dark of night, seize knives and slit their throats as they slept. Treasured ayahs, who had been as second mothers to British children, found they were not allowed out of the sight of their particular memsahibs with their young charges.

And this suspicion reaped a bitter harvest, for those who knew they were no longer trusted, even when they were fiercely loyal, began to resent this doubt, and to wonder if, perhaps, their loyalties would be better placed elsewhere.

None of this, of course, was known to Emily, eating breakfast in the privacy of her room on that first morning, but it was gleaned easily enough simply by listening to conversations around her, by using her eyes and ears normally in the household in which she was staying. And Simone, of course, was an inveterate passer-on of gossip, in whatever environment she found herself.

The Smythe family's summer residence was a spacious bungalow set in its own elegant grounds, and Emily's bedroom had once been occupied by one of the daughters now in England. A small room, once a dressing-room or study nearby, was allotted to Simone Looking at her surroundings that morning, Emily could well have imagined herself in England, and the furnishings throughout the house confirmed that illusion. It was a cherished and comforting illusion to almost every Anglo-Indian family, who found something solid and reassuring about their horsehair sofas and heavy mahogany furniture. But Emily was homesick for Bilkhondar, for the silken divans and silver lamps, the marble pillars and ever-reflecting pools, for the real East that she had known and come to love.

The house had a cool verandah, amply provided with cane furniture, to which she escaped as often as she could, to sit in a quiet corner and look out on the garden. But it was essentially an English garden with beds of orderly roses and carefully watered lawns, and here, there were no fountains.

Sometimes, on waking early in the morning, before she had fully emerged from the confusion of sleep, Emily thought she heard them, splashing coolly into the marble basins. She would turn over, lazily, running her hand over the warm indentation left by Dara's body in the bed, but her fingers encountered only the crisply laundered sheet on which she slept alone. And there were no fountains.

She received nothing but kindness and thoughtful attention from Mrs. Smythe, a tall woman with an ample, stately figure, and traces of youthful prettiness still lingering in her face, and in the auburn hair, now streaked with grey, which must once have been glorious. Meals were planned with the specific purpose of building up Emily, who was too thin by half, her hostess decided.

The very first day, the dressmaker was sent for, and both Emily and Simone were measured for new clothes, which were made up in great haste, since neither of them had anything suitable to wear.

Emily found them uncomfortable and constricting, these complicated European clothes, with their tight corsets and intricate fastenings. She found it difficult to gauge the precise amount of space required to negotiate furniture and doorways in the unaccustomed crinoline, after the sinuous rustling silks of her saris. The habits of a lifetime, forgotten in a few short months!

"You should be greatly pleased – pregnancy has done almost nothing to your waistline," Simone noted, lacing up Emily's stays.

"My waistline is of no great consequence," Emily replied, aware of a sensation akin to panic rising within her. "What worries me is my mind – my heart. I cannot stay here, Simone. I cannot be wholly a European woman again. It is all play-acting. Under the skin, I am something quite different."

"Hush, *ma petite*. You have to stay here, since there is nowhere else for you to go," Simone said reasonably. "If you do your play-acting well enough, for long enough, it will one day become real."

"I doubt it. The springs are broken somewhere, Simone, and can't be mended. Even if they could, what would be the object of it?"

"To live, *chérie*. To survive. One day, you will find a purpose."

"Not here, I shall not. There, in the harem, while there was danger for the girls, it still seemed to matter, but here – I wish I were dead, Simone, that's what I wish. Why am I not dead?"

"You must not say that! It is sinful," Simone crossed herself, a habit she had suppressed without difficulty in the harem, but here in Poona, she had suddenly decided to become an ardent Catholic once more.

"Sinful!" Emily glared at the pile of starched petticoats waiting to be put on. "It is sinful for me to be alive whilst Dara is dead. It is criminal to expect me to live on for another fifty or sixty years without him. I can't do it, Simone, I can't."

She paced the room, silently, then came to an abrupt halt. "Unlace me again, please, Simone, then would you be good enough to tell Mrs. Smythe I am a little indisposed, and ask her if I may be excused from joining her for dinner tonight."

Alone, she wrapped herself in the peignoir left behind by one of the Smythe girls, who must have been a fairly hefty girl, since it hung loosely round Emily' now reed-slim body. She looked thoughtfully at herself in the dressing-table mirror, and to aid the half-formed thoughts in her head, began to brush her long hair out of the ringlets into which Simone had carefully tortured it.

As she brushed and gazed, the thoughts gradually coalesced and formed themselves into words. I am condemned and sentenced, she said to herself, why should I not be my own executioner? She was suffering, needlessly, when freedom was such a simple thing. If it were true what believing people of all religions said, she could be reunited with Dara in death. If it were not, as her sharply critical mind sometimes suspected, then at least she would be released from this futile and painful existence.

She had brought only two things out of Bilkhondar with her. One was the silver inscribed ring, which she wore at all times, even though she had seen Mrs. Smythe casting odd glances at it. The other was the ceremonial jewelled dagger, the one Prince Dara had worn in his belt the last time he came to see her, the one he had thrown to the floor at her feet, before riding out into that fateful night. A symbol of his good faith, he had called it. Now it should be a symbol of her emancipation.

Her eyes glittered as she withdrew the dagger from the drawer where it lay, looking alien and out of place among the paraphernalia of a Victorian lady's bedroom. The blade appeared cruel enough, and she tested it experimentally against her finger. Blood spurted brightly from the cut, and she licked it, tasting the saltiness of it on her tongue. Silly to worry about a bloodstain on a borrowed wrap, when one was about to put an end to one's life. She smiled at herself in the mirror. There was no fear, such as she had known when Prince Murad's guards had drawn their swords, only a slight anxiety that she should find the correct spot and plunge the knife sufficiently deep, that she should do it properly and not bungle it.

She closed her eyes, took several deep breaths, and raised the dagger, holding it firmly in both hands. So absolute was her concentration that she did not hear the door of her bedroom opening. She knew nothing until she felt firm hands grasping her wrists, and wrenching the dagger from her.

Emily opened her eyes, and Mrs. Smythe's face swam before them. She had been in a state of semi-trance, and it took a while for the room to come into focus again.

"You foolish girl!" the other woman scolded her, in the tone of mingled anger and relief a mother uses to a child whose mischief has caused it a narrow escape from injury. She passed the dagger to Simone, who was hovering anxiously in the doorway, and said briskly, "Fetch the brandy from the cupboard downstairs. I don't believe in smelling salts in a case such as this."

She rubbed Emily's nerveless hands until some warmth returned to them. In her mind, the girl had counted herself already dead, and she found it difficult to accept that her attempt had been foiled, and here she was, still, with all her problems unsolved. Simone brought the brandy, and the Colonel's wife insisted that Emily drink some. She forced it down, almost choking, but the colour came back to her cheeks, and her eyes lost their glazed, faraway look.

"Leave us, now," Mrs. Smythe said to Simone, and as the French girl hesitated, she added gently, "Your perceptiveness and your quick action in telling me what you suspected, have saved her life, and I thank you. Miss Hunter will be all right, but now she and I have some talking to do."

Simone acquiesced, and closed the door behind her,

and Mrs. Smythe persuaded Emily to lie down on the bed. Then she drew up a chair beside her and sat down.

"That was an exceedingly silly thing you tried to do, just now," she said, matter of factly.

"It did not seem so to me," Emily said wearily, "and I very much regret your having prevented me."

"My dear girl!" Mrs. Smythe's voice gained a shade in irritation. "*You* may regret it, but I do not. I cannot have young ladies committing suicide in my house."

Emily's smile was slightly ironic. "No, of course, I realise it was fearfully ill-mannered of me, after you have received me as your guest," she said. "But I didn't plan it, it just came to me, and moreover, I have nowhere else to go."

"What nonsense you talk!" said the Colonel's wife. "Nor do I want you to go killing yourself elsewhere, in order to spare my clean sheets and my reputation! My child, I know, from what my husband wrote to me, that terrible things have happened to you, but you must not feel that death is the only way out."

"Isn't it?"

"Of course not. You must try to forget, must begin to live again. After all, no one knows, here in Poona, about how you spent the past year, and they shall not learn of it from me or from my husband. Certain of my friends know that I have a house-guest, a young lady who was living in a princely state to the south, and has escaped from the mutineers. That is all they know."

Emily rose on her elbow.

"But I have nothing to hide," she said. "Do I have to be secretive, to lie about what happened to me?"

"For your own good, my dear. Can you not see that? The Press would have a wonderful time with your story, should we allow it to leak out, and you would not want it splashed all over the front pages, would you?"

"No," Emily admitted.

"Besides, there is your future to consider. When you are well again, and feeling more like yourself, we can introduce you into society. There will be young men – at least, there will if this dreadful uprising spares us. Some day, you will want to marry."

Emily was sitting upright in bed, now, her expression horrified.

"That is quite out of the question," she said, more sharply than she had intended. "You cannot introduce a harem woman into polite society. You cannot expect any of your friends' sons to marry me, unless they are prepared to behave like the man who married Teresa Guiccioli, and went about introducing her as 'my wife, Lord Byron's former mistress'. Didn't Colonel Smythe tell you about my life in Bilkhondar?"

Mrs. Smythe looked at the counterpane, and then back at Emily.

"He told me you had been taken as the concubine of an Indian prince, and that you had had a stillborn child. My dear, I have been married more than twenty years, and have borne two children of my own. I can imagine how terrible this experience must have been for you. But why should you be penalised for the rest of your life, for something over which you had no choice?"

Emily met the other woman's eyes candidly. This was a good woman, understanding up to a point, and sympathetic. She had been calm and collected over her guest's attempted suicide, she had refused to be disturbed by her recently colourful past. But, like her husband, she had not fully grasped the reality of the situation, and now she was going to have to, and she was going to be shocked, for Emily was not prepared to dissemble over it.

"I had a choice," she said. "Prince Dara was not the

kind of man who would force his attentions on a woman – not the kind of man who needed to. I loved him. I was willingly his, and I am not ashamed of it. I shall never love anyone else, and I shall certainly never marry."

Mrs. Smythe stood up. She *was* shocked, that was obvious, although she was trying not to show it. Emily's revelations had opened up a rift between them which could not be crossed. Her sympathy had been for a young English lady, forced against her will to become the mistress of a native prince. To this brazen woman, who confessed she had gone into the affair with her eyes open, she could not, try as she might, extend that same sympathy.

"If you will take my advice, you will keep those sentiments to yourself, for you will hardly find them fashionable in India, especially at the present time," she said, unconsciously echoing her husband in the way that long-married people often did. "I shall have your dinner sent up to you on a tray, since you are not feeling well. Will you give me your word that you will make no further attempts upon your life?"

Emily smiled wanly. "Not while I am under your roof, I promise," she said.

Simone came in later, took away Emily's untouched dinner, and brought her some tea.

"Stay with me a while," Emily said. "You did me no service, this evening, but you are still the only friend I have."

"*Tiens!* I could not let you kill yourself! Without you, I have no purpose in this household. Why should they keep me?" Simone perched on the edge of the bed, and poured herself some tea. "The memsahib is a little cool towards you, I sense."

"Oh, it is not her fault," Emily sighed. "I told her – I had to tell her – that I loved Dara freely, and of my own choice, otherwise she was ready to marry me off to some pink-faced subaltern, fresh from England, who was to be misled about my history. It is no good, Simone. I know, and now the Colonel's wife also knows, that I can never again fit easily into British Society. There is nothing else for me, but to go back to Bilkhondar."

Simone's eyes flew wide open. "But how? And even if you could get there, what would you do?"

"I don't know. There has been fighting, there must be people who need nursing, there is terrible poverty and disease in Bilkhondar, to begin with. If I must live, then I must do something useful."

"You have no money, *chérie*. And nothing you can sell to raise money – except Prince Dara's ring."

Emily looked down at her hand. "That has more sentiment than value," she said. "I left jewellery more valuable behind in the harem. Besides, I would not part with it. Oh, I do not know the answer, Simone, but I shall find some way. And don't worry – I shan't ask you to go with me if you don't wish to. Mrs. Smythe will soon find you another position."

"Ah, bah!" said Simone. "We shall talk of that when we have to. In the meantime, you would do well to get some sleep."

She did not sleep for a long time, but lay plotting and planning, trying to find a way for a woman, without help or money, to make her way across a country prepared for possible war. And to find a means for a purposeful existence once there. She was no nearer a solution when she finally fell asleep.

She was in her room next morning with Simone, who had just finished helping her to dress, when, with a light tap on the door, Mrs. Smythe herself walked in.

"Ah, I see you are dressed," she said. "Would you please come downstairs into the drawing room, Mis-

Hunter. There is a message from my husband in Bil-khondar, and I imagine it must be important, since he has sent his second-in-command to deliver it."

Emily went quickly and lightly downstairs, where she found the smartly-uniformed Major awaiting her. Time and distance had done nothing to alleviate the instinctive antagonism between them, but oddly enough, because he had come from Bilkhondar, she was pleased to see him.

"Good morning, Major."

"Miss Hunter." He gave a precise little bow. "I trust you are well?"

"Well enough, thank you."

Never one to waste much time on pleasantries, he said, "Can you be ready to travel within the hour? My orders are to escort you to Bilkhondar."

To his amazement, Emily bestowed on him a radiant smile. "Why, Major Hargreaves," she said, "I never thought I should say so, but you really are the answer to a maiden's prayer."

She could elicit no further information from him as to the purpose of the Colonel's summons; he could not, or would not, say how long the sojourn was expected to be. Emily changed quickly into her newly-made riding habit, and had Simone pack a few essentials, since the Major had forbidden any baggage that would impede their progress. He cavilled at having to take Simone along with them, since she had not distinguished her-self as a horsewoman on the outward journey, and horseback was the only possible way to make the rough ascent into Bilkhondar, where roads scarcely existed.

"Miss Hunter can scarcely make such a journey with you, unchaperoned," Mrs. Smythe said reprovingly. "I am sure my husband would not expect her to."

"I don't know, ma'am. He gave no instructions,

other than to bring Miss Hunter to Bilkhóndar as swiftly as possible. More I cannot say, since matters of security are involved."

The Colonel's wife gave him a withering look. "I understand the situation perfectly, young man. I have been a senior officer's wife for too long to require instruction. But Miss Hunter is a young, single lady, and she cannot travel with you without her personal maid. I have ordered both their horses saddled."

The Major's insolent eyes said plainly enough that he did not consider Emily had any virtue worth guarding from him, but he acquiesced, somewhat ungraciously.

Mrs. Smythe embraced Emily with unexpected warmth. "I have no idea what this is about, my child, but my home will be here for you, should you need it," she said.

"Thank you," Emily replied. "I am sorry to have been such a trouble to you. I wish we could have met in happier circumstances."

"She is glad to see the backs of us," Simone commented, as they rode away.

"No doubt. And who can blame her?" Emily responded.

By hard riding, and minimal stops for rest and meals they made the return journey with remarkable speed The heat was oppressive, and the Major made no allowances for it, although Simone complained loudly and incessantly.

Emily said little, and made no protest about the speed or the conditions of their journey. She was a eager as Hargreaves to reach Bilkhondar, and ever mile which brought her nearer was welcomed. She could not imagine why the Colonel had sent for her – al she could assume was that there was some way she could assist him in his dealings with the harem – but that would hardly account for the urgency involved, particularly when he had sent her away, so firmly, such a short time ago. In a way, his reasons hardly mattered to her; she was curious, but not overly concerned. What was important was that she was going back, as she had yearned to do, and this time she did not intend to be so easily dislodged.

The heat lessened slightly as they began to ride into the hills, and Emily saw the jagged black peaks of the Ghats etched against the blinding blue of the sky. A feeling of homecoming washed over her, the nearest thing to gladness she had known since Dara's death, and she spurred her horse onwards over the rough ground, leaving the Major to catch up with her, and Simone grumbling loudly at the rear. Through the half-ruined city, now just beginning to recover a little from the onslaught of invasion, through the narrow, winding streets of the bazaars, where ragged children scattered before them, anxious to get out of the way, and people watched from the shadow of doorways. Through the immense gates, which opened at the Major's sharply barked command, and into the main courtyard. Instinctively, Emily's gaze flew to the marble grillework high above, where she sensed, rather than saw, women's eyes looking down at her.

The Colonel had set up his headquarters in Prince Murad's great audience hall; there were makeshift desks everywhere, and men marching in and out on this duty or the other. Major Hargreaves led Emily into a small chamber at the back of the hall, which was clearly the hub of what was now a military garrison, and where the Colonel sat behind a table strewn with maps and papers.

He rose as they entered, and smiled at Emily. She thought he looked tired and harassed.

"My dear girl – so we meet again, sooner than I had anticipated," he said. "A chair for Miss Hunter, Major, and then you may leave us."

"Indeed, Colonel," said Emily, when they were alone, "you seemed most anxious to have me safely in Poona; now I must return to Bilkhondar again. I confess myself greatly puzzled."

"And I am most apologetic. But it was necessary, as you shall see. First, though – how is my wife? And Poona?"

"Mrs. Smythe is well. As for Poona, I have seen little of it, but as you can imagine, there is much concern about the Mutiny. Poona is quiet, Colonel, but far from easy."

He nodded. "As I would have expected. I have just this morning received news that Cawnpore has fallen. The Nana Sahib, who I believe was a friend of Prince Murad, offered the survivors of the garrison safe passage to Allahabad along the river, and massacred them all as they were boarding the boats."

Emily blanched. "Is it never going to end, this horror?" she asked.

"Not yet, I fear, since violence breeds violence," the Colonel replied. "There is a man called Neill who has blazed his way to Allahabad, hanging and shooting everything that moves, burning villages about the ears of the inhabitants. The repercussions of this summer, Emily, will be a long time dying."

Tea was brought in, and Emily, from long habit of acting hostess, took off her gloves and poured. The Colonel watched her, soberly.

"You will have need of that," he told her, deliberately waiting as she set the cup back on its saucer. "We have found your Prince Dara."

She looked at him, her face drained of colour. "You

mean – you have found his body?" she said bitterly. "Is that why I have been brought from Poona, to identify him?"

"Use your sense, girl," he said tersely. "A body putrefies within the day in this climate. Those killed in battle were buried before nightfall the same day, which, as you must know, is the custom here. We have found Prince Dara – alive."

Emily clutched the edge of the table so hard that her knuckles turned white. She tried to speak, but found her throat dry. She stood up, sat down again, and found that the Colonel had produced a bottle of brandy from somewhere. In the midst of her distraction, she noted again the way he and his wife followed similar lines of action in a crisis, as if marriage produced a coalition of thought-processes. And once again, the fiery liquid burned her throat, and restored her senses.

"I don't understand," she said faintly. "Dara alive? How can that be?"

"A great deal can happen in the confusion of fighting," the Colonel said. "Until you informed me, I had no idea the Prince was involved in the action, nor had any of the men who were present. According to our intelligence, most lamentably, he was still in England. It was assumed within the palace that he was killed in action?"

"Yes, because his horse came back riderless – and anyhow, he was not in action, I told you, he rode out to try and prevent it." Emily stood up, and began to pace the small room, agitatedly. "If Dara is alive, where is he? I want to see him. I shan't believe it until I do."

"In time, my dear, in time," the Colonel said soothingly. "He is not here, he is at a summer palace in the hills, so you cannot see him yet. Sit down, drink your tea, and let us piece together what happened."

She obeyed, still too numbed by the news to have assimilated the full import of it.

"He was shot down by a stray bullet, as we assumed, but after the battle was over, one of Prince Murad's retainers who had ridden with him, and somehow managed to avoid capture, returned to the battlefield at night and found the Prince, wounded and unconscious."

The Colonel put a hand over Emily's, as he saw she was about to jump up again. "Calm yourself, he is in no danger, now, from the injuries he received. This man who rescued him was afraid to bring him into the city."

"And rightly so," Emily said grimly. "He would have received scant assistance for the Prince on that day."

Colonel Smythe inclined his head.

"You are never going to forget that, are you?" he said.

"That I saw my countrymen behaving like savages? No, never," she answered steadily. "But I know you were not personally responsible, so I will try to stop reminding you of it. I am sorry, Please go on."

"The man and his wife took Prince Dara to the old summer palace and cared for him as best they could. Apparently the place is deserted and has not been used for some time. But the Prince had suffered a gunshot wound in the shoulder, and without proper medical knowledge, they could do nothing for him. He was near to death, so in the end, it was the woman who came to the city, seeking help. It must have taken considerable courage for her to do so."

"Indeed it must. This was while I was in Poona?"

"Shortly after you left. But still, you see, she did not betray the identity of the man they were tending, simply said he had been wounded in battle."

"She came to you?"

"No. To my military surgeon, who arrived in Bilkhondar with me. She was fortunate in her choice. He is a man who cares for human lives, irrespective of which side they fight for. He spent three days and three nights at the summer palace, and undoubtedly, he saved the Prince's life. To what end, I am not sure."

"What do you mean?" Emily demanded apprehensively.

The Colonel shook his head, and shifted the papers on his desk uneasily.

"We have here the son of a rebel prince who was killed in action against us. You say he took no part in that action, and I am prepared to believe you. Still, he is . . . who he is, and I am not rightly sure what is to be done with him."

"What does Prince Dara himself say?" she countered. "Have you spoken to him?"

"Once. He has said remarkably little; in fact, he seems supremely unconcerned as to whether he lives or dies. Supremely unconcerned about anything, I would say."

"Dara? No, that cannot be. He was . . . is a passionate man, with strong opinions. Are you *sure* this man is Prince Dara?"

"At first we had no idea, although it was obvious from his dress that he was at least of the nobility. He was in delirium, and spoke no language that my surgeon understood, but here and there came a word of English, so we guessed he was western-educated. Not until he recovered his senses did we learn his identity. By his own confession, he is the son of Prince Murad."

Emily buried her face in her hands. It was all too much for her to take in. First of all, the incredible news that Dara, whom she had believed dead for over a month, was actually still alive, then this fantastic story of his rescue and hairsbreadth recovery from his wounds. Finally, and disturbingly, the report of his apparent indifference to life, and the unpleasant question-mark hanging over his future.

"But what can you do to him – of what is he guilty?" she cried, lifting her head to look at him once more.

"Of being the son of an insurgent, and the descendant of a Mogul dynasty," he replied. "Do I have to remind you that Delhi is still under siege, and the mutineers who ransacked the city, killing every British man, woman and child they could lay hands on, did so in the name of the Mogul emperor? A cipher, maybe, but a rallying point, and a danger. Can you be sure that Bilkhondar will not attempt to rise again, under Prince Dara?"

"The Prince Dara I knew would never subject the helpless, poverty-stricken people of Bilkhondar to further useless bloodshed," she retorted.

"Not even to avenge his father's death? Can you be sure?" the Colonel repeated grimly. "Emily, I should have this young man at least put under lock and key for many years, in the deepest, safest dungeon I can find. In my position, Major Hargreaves would doubtless prefer a more permanent solution. Two things stayed my hand. One is that so far no one, apart from the couple who cared for him, and my surgeon and myself knows that he is alive."

"Not even the Major?" Emily let out a long breath of relief.

"Least of all him, although I am sure he is wondering why I had you brought back post-haste from Poona."

"You said two things. What was the other one?" she asked.

"My belief that you had some . . . affection for th

Prince," he replied carefully. "Correct me if I am wrong."

Emily saw that she had previously judged this man a little too hastily, when she thought he did not understand how things were.

"I loved him – still love him – above everything," she replied simply.

"The more I thought about it, the more my mind was forced to that conclusion. And having met him, briefly – well, he is a most personable young man."

"Oh, he is more than that," Emily breathed. "Colonel Smythe, you surely cannot put Dara in prison for years. He is an active man, both mentally and physically, and to be thus confined would be torture to him. He would rather be dead."

"At the moment, he is showing no propensity towards any kind of activity," the Colonel said. "My surgeon says he may well be suffering from delayed shock, that he may yet come round and react violently to what has taken place. This is a sick man, my dear, and I warn you, almost certainly not the man you remember."

"Oh yes, yes," Emily cried impatiently. "I realise that. But may I see him? *When* may I see him?"

"When you have rested. Tomorrow, you can be taken to the summer palace. In fact, Emily, the solution I have in mind for this complicated problem depends entirely on you. Without you, it falls to the ground and I have no alternative to a long prison sentence."

"What can I do? Only tell me?" She asked urgently.

The Colonel looked intently at her, across the table, observing her slightest reaction. "Would you be prepared to marry him?" he said.

"Would I be prepared . . . ?" She gave an incredul-

ous laugh. To be married to him! Something which, in
their time together, she had accepted as an impossibil-
ity, and now here was this man, offering her this prize
on a plate, no, asking it of her, as a precondition for
Dara's freedom.

"Gladly," she said. "Would it help, if he were married to me?"

"I believe so. You are a British subject, and therefore
it is less likely that he will offer violence to your compatriots. You must appreciate, Emily, that what I am
asking of you is virtually that you guarantee his good
behaviour during these troubled times. I see no other
way for him. He cannot reign in Bilkhondar. For the
moment, you and he would not be acceptable in India.
But with an allowance, you could live comfortably and
quietly in the summer palace. Could you agree to that?
Would he?"

"Does he have any choice?" she said, a slow anger
stirring within her. "For myself, I could ask for no
more. In any event, Colonel, as Mrs. Smythe will surely
tell you, I cannot be part of British society any more;
there is no going back to that. I discovered as much in
Poona. I would do anything for Prince Dara, and what
you are asking of me is –" she laughed, a trifle nervously, "is really not very onerous."

"Very well." The Colonel, once assured of her essential agreement, became brisk and businesslike.
"Tonight you will stay here. I shall have a room prepared for you."

"There is no need. I already have rooms here."

"I know. But you cannot stay in the harem. Your
presence would arouse too much comment and specula-
tion. This marriage must take place quickly, Emily, if
at all, and as few people as possible must know of it
beforehand. I must ask you particularly not to tell yo

maid any of this. She is a good girl, but talks too much."

"Simone has been with me all through this. It will be difficult to keep her in the dark."

"But necessary, I'm afraid. I do not want word of this spreading through the palace and the city like wildfire. What we are doing is presenting it as a *fait accompli*. You will ride to the summer palace tomorrow morning, accompanied by your maid and my surgeon, who will act as witnesses to the ceremony."

"And you?" she said, beginning to feel a little fearful. "Where will you be?"

"Here, attending to my business," he said, "so that I do not need to be too deeply involved in this, nor arouse suspicion by my absence."

Emily fidgeted in her seat. "But surely, Colonel, you are not expecting me to propose to Prince Dara?" she said. "You must see that I cannot, even though I love him, even after all we have been to one another."

He smiled. "So there is still a trace of the modest English miss beneath all your exterior unconventionality," he said, not unkindly. "Do not fear. My chaplain will ride out early in the morning, and he will talk to the Prince on my behalf, and explain the situation to him. If he is a reasonable young man, he will not be slow to understand how things are, and if he loves you, he should not be difficult to persuade."

That night, once again, Emily lay within the walls of the palace of Bilkhondar, although not in the harem. Simone, who shared the vigil with her, was deeply suspicious of the whole affair.

"Are we prisoners here, you and I?" she demanded. I only wanted to visit my old friends in the women's quarters, but that sergeant outside the door physically prevented me. I know the Colonel does not think it fitting for you to stay inside the harem, but what harm would it do to have a chat with some of the girls?"

"No, we are not prisoners," Emily reassured her, "but for tonight, the Colonel has asked that we stay here. Tomorrow you will see why," she promised.

Simone's eyes were resentful.

"You know something, and you will not tell me," she accused.

"*Cannot* tell you. The Colonel asked for my word that I would tell no one. Please trust me, Simone. We are in no danger, and tomorrow, all will be well."

"*Tiens!* Since there is nothing else I can do. . . ." The French girl lifted her shoulders in a little shrug of disgust.

Emily tried to sleep. She tried sincerely and hard, for tomorrow she was to see Dara again, whom she had thought dead, and gone from her for ever. It was like a miracle, it *was* a miracle, for his life had hung, like a slender thread, depending on so many strange circumstances. If the man had not returned to the battlefield, if his wife had been too afraid to seek help, if the surgeon had been less than sympathetic and dedicated . . . and even now, his fate, his safety, depended on her, upon Emily Hunter from Overhampton.

She closed her eyes and breathed deeply, and prayed for sleep to come. It alone could silence her increasing agitation, and besides, she would not have been woman had she not been concerned to look her best. But she could only doze fitfully, torn by her anxiety for his state of health, her natural apprehension about the marriage, and her intense longing to see him again. Once she saw him, was with him, heard his voice, touched his hand, she was convinced that all would be resolved. Until then, there was only the endless night and the interminable waiting.

CHAPTER
NINE

THE muezzin's call awoke her from the light sleep into which she had eventually fallen, and she listened to it with a kind of wonder, reminiscent of her first long-ago morning in Bilkhondar. The sun was high and bright in the sky, and already it was hot. Today is my wedding-day, she thought.

She bathed, and dressed carefully in her riding habit once more, since she had nothing else suitable for a journey into the hills. Simone dressed her hair European fashion, swept up high on her head, with carefully contrived ringlets and tendrils.

"I don't know about that," Emily said, looking doubtfully at herself in the glass.

"*Mais si*, of course, it has to be like that, to suit the clothes," protested Simone. "Am I to be told where we are going?"

"Into the hills, on horseback," Emily replied vaguely.

"Ouch – *pas encore!* I am heartily sick of horses," complained the French girl. "But in that case, the hair must be taken up, to keep it in place whilst riding."

"I suppose so," Emily acquiesced reluctantly. She must play the English lady for a few more hours, and after that, she need no longer pretend.

After an early breakfast, Colonel Smythe arrived, accompanied by a thin, fair-haired, moustached young man whom he introduced as his surgeon, Captain Carruthers.

Emily returned his handclasp warmly. "So it was you, I understand, who saved Prince Dara's life," she said. "There is nothing I can say to you which would adequately express my feelings. 'Thank you' would sound too trite."

He had an open, engaging smile, which would have endeared him to her, whoever he was.

"But sufficient, I think. I did what I would have done for anyone, and I was aided by luck and the gentleman's own strength."

"You are too modest," Emily said.

The Colonel broke in on them with a polite cough.

"You should leave now, before the sun becomes too oppressive," he told them. He gave Emily a swift fatherly embrace. "Good luck, my dear, and my best wishes to you." He was surprised, but not altogether displeased, when Emily stood on tiptoe and kissed him on the cheek.

"And thank you, dear Colonel Smythe, for all you have done," she said.

"I have only made the arrangements," he insisted. "*You* must do the rest. Are you quite sure it is what you wish to do? Even now, it is not too late for you to change your mind."

"Oh no, I am quite sure," she said.

Simone rode abreast with her as they cantered out. Her eyes were like saucers.

"What was all that, just now?" she probed. "I did not overhear all of it, but I could have sworn you said Prince Dara was alive."

Emily turned a radiant face towards her. "He is – and I am going to him. Isn't it wonderful?"

As they climbed higher into the hills, the going

became rougher, and they needed all their concentration to guide their horses and prevent them from stumbling. At least, Simone and the doctor did. Mr. Scrooge appeared remarkably sure-footed, and Emily thought how often Dara had ridden him among these same hills. She told herself it was fanciful, but he seemed to know where they were going.

For several hours, they made their way steadily upwards. The Captain was a considerate guide, and stopped frequently for them to rest, but Emily was impatient of the delay, and she was always the first to remount. Maybe it was indelicate for a potential bride to be so eager to reach her bridegroom, but she no longer cared about appearances. Dara was waiting, that was what mattered.

At length, they came out on to a high, level plateau, almost surrounded by higher mountains, and she had her first sight of the summer palace. She thought it was mis-named, for it was a squat, square, fortress-like building, with huge wooden doors, and slit-eyed windows that betrayed nothing of the interior.

"Built to resist marauding tribesmen," said Captain Carruthers, noting her brief hesitation. "You will find it less grim from the inside."

He dismounted and thumped heartily upon the thick doors, obviously unnecessarily, since their approach could not, from that direction, have been made unnoticed. The door was creaked open almost at once by a middle-aged man, who bowed to Emily with deference, but not servility.

She thought quickly, which language would he speak? He had ridden out as a retainer of Prince Murad, and could be a noble in his own right, not a servant, although he had chosen to devote himself to the injured Prince. She took a chance, paid a compliment to his

rank and addressed him in Persian, speaking of her
gratitude and admiration for all he and his wife had
done.

His eyes lit up, and he replied that his name was
Yusuf Khan, his wife was called Nargis, and they were
honoured to serve Prince Dara and the Lady Nadira.
His wife materialised out of the dimness of the interior,
and, smiling, invited Emily by gesture not simply to
enter, but to take possession. Captain Carruthers, who
had clearly not understood a word of this, but had
grasped the underlying sentiments, stood aside to allow
Emily to go inside, followed by Simone, carrying the
small valise. Yusuf led the horses away to be stabled.

Following Nargis along the dark corridor, Emily
caught glimpses of light and greenery ahead, and as
they drew nearer to the source of it, she realised that the
place was built around a large, central courtyard and
garden. The garden was rampant and overgrown, but
the fountain in the centre was working, triumphantly
asserting the Muslim builders' aesthetic demands for
living water in all their designs.

Nargis paused outside a door, upon which she rapped lightly. No voice granted them admission, but she
smiled and held the door open.

"The Prince is here?" Emily asked, her knees shaking beneath the demure skirt of her habit, and her
hands suddenly cold with perspiration. The woman
nodded, and stood waiting for Emily to pass.

Captain Carruthers smiled encouragingly.

"I will go and find the chaplain – he is a student of
foreign flora, and will no doubt be investigating the
gardens," he said. "Let us know when you need us.
Perhaps your maid will go with you."

"Yes. Please," Emily said, clutching Simone's hand.
Meeting Dara again was, in a sense, like encountering

someone risen from the dead, and she had need of her friend's solid, pragmatic presence.

Nargis closed the door behind them. It was a large room, in shadow beside the door where they stood, but bright towards the far end, where full-length doors stood open to the gardens. The floors were pure, clean marble, but the rugs spread on them, although luxurious, showed signs of age and wear, and so did all the furnishings, emphasising the atmosphere of decay and dilapidation which hung about this strange building.

At first, Emily thought Nargis had been mistaken, and the room was quite empty apart from themselves. Then she saw the figure of a man, standing framed in the doorway to the garden, very still and with his back to them, one hand resting against the framework of the door, his head bent in contemplation. If he heard them enter, he made no move.

Simone sank on to a carved stool just inside the entrance to the room. "I am here, *chérie*, but further I cannot go with you," she whispered.

Emily smiled, and walked slowly towards where the man was standing, her skirts murmuring against the cool marble of the floor. Halfway there, she stopped abruptly, and began pulling off her gloves.

He must have been aware of her presence, for he turned to face her, and it *was* Dara, miraculously alive and real. He had lost weight, the splendid physique somewhat wasted by illness, even his face appeared thinner, emphasising more strongly the fine, Mogul features. But he was alive, and it was enough.

Over and above all she had endured, the emotion of this moment almost overcame her. Poised to run to him, she saw his eyes, and the expression in them was sufficient to stop her dead in her tracks.

There was no warmth in them, no feeling whatsoever, beyond a kind of gentle irony. He looked at her as one might regard a figure from one's distant past, as if he had forgotten that such a short time ago, they had been lovers, as if all that belonged to a different age.

"Ah, Emily," he said, in a cool, polite voice. "You are well, I see." There was in his attitude a slight, princely condescension she had never known in him before, as though, now all that was gone, he was more than ever conscious of the long, illustrious lineage stretching back to Akbar and to Tamerlane.

She, who had coped resourcefully with so many bizarre and frightening events, so many difficult situations, was at a loss to know how to deal with this calm, indifferent Dara. She longed to throw herself into his arms, but she did not dare. One look at his face told her that such excessive emotionalism would be unwelcome, might even be distasteful.

"Thank you, yes," she said, trying to control the tremor in her own voice. She watched his face as she added nervously, "I lost the child – did you know? I am sorry."

Something flickered briefly in his eyes, but his face did not alter as he said, "Yusuf Khan told me. I am sorry, too – sorry that you should ever have found yourself in such circumstances."

She wanted to shout, to beat her hands against his chest, to scream at him to stop this nonsense. But she could not. That icy, unmoving expression of his was like a cold hand on her heart. He was denying all they had been to each other, and she could not bear it.

He made a bored gesture towards the overgrown gardens.

"Would you believe, this place was built as a love nest by one of my ancestors, who ran off with a woman his family found unsuitable," he said. "Hardly worth the trouble, I should have thought, since he had to spend most of his time defending it from the hill tribes."

"What . . . what happened to the woman?" Emily asked, with attempted lightness.

"What? Oh, I believe she died in childbirth soon after her arrival. The place has fallen into considerable disrepair, as you can see. Perhaps that makes it a highly suitable abode for myself." A brittle laugh, which did not quite hide the depths of bitterness. His eyes raked over her neatly fitting riding habit, the high-piled curls of her hairstyle. "Poona seems to have been highly suitable for you," he said.

"On the contrary," she said levelly. "I did not care for it at all. Otherwise I should have stayed there."

He inclined his head, his slight smile awarding her the point. "And now we are to be united in holy wedlock, you and I, with the kind permission of Colonel Smythe, military commander of Bilkhondar."

"Not if you do not wish it," she said, her head high, her whole body rigid.

"One would be discourteous to refuse," he said. He walked past her, his footsteps echoing across the empty spaces of the room. "Simone, be good enough to tell Captain Carruthers we are ready."

A small, angry devil of wounded pride and rejection urged Emily to shout, no! Not like this! I shall go back to Poona, and you can rot in the deepest dungeon in Bilkhondar for all I care! She resisted it. She had made her commitment when the Colonel had first put the proposition to her, and she was not going to renege on it now, simply because their reunion had not been the romantic consummation she had desired. The alternative for Dara was still the same, a limitless term of imprisonment, and whilst he might not at the moment care one way or the other, she still cared very much.

She had a notion that if she did what her pride dictated, he would accept prison as indifferently as he accepted marriage. More than that, by his offhand treatment of her, she thought he was goading her to leave him to his fate. Perhaps he saw this end as a suitable punishment for his failure to influence the course of events.

Recalling what the doctor had said about his mental condition, she bit her tongue and forced herself to remain calm. If she were going to have to save him in spite of himself, then so be it. She could endure it. She seemed to have discovered a fatal talent for endurance, she thought ruefully.

And so she went through her marriage ceremony like a somnambulist, wishing it could all be a bad dream from which she would soon awake. Prince Dara's cutting, "I am nominally a Muslim, you know. Could you not obtain the services of the Imam?" The chaplain's quiet, dignified apology. "I am sorry, it was a risk we dared not take, for security reasons. I assure you, the marriage will be legal."

"Perhaps we could have the Muslim ceremony at a later date," Emily interposed.

"My wife-to-be is unfailingly resourceful," murmured Prince Dara.

The chaplain coughed, embarrassed. He had understood this to be a love-match, but he saw nothing in the behaviour of this young man to confirm this, and the bride was pale and tense. "Let us begin," he said.

The witnesses stood grave-faced and silent. Emily repeated her marriage vows in a clear, calm voice, and Dara did not falter once throughout the ceremony, albeit strange to him. To have and to hold from this day forward, for better for worse, for richer for poorer, in sickness and in health. . . . Emily wondered if she would ever again have the Dara she had known in Bilkhondar, who had filled her days and nights with love and laughter and excitement, or if she would spend her life here, in this isolated spot, with this withdrawn and occasionally sarcastic man.

The chaplain pronounced them man and wife, and Dara's lips brushed Emily's cheek in a perfunctory kiss.

Simone's embrace was wholehearted, although her eyes were troubled. *"Bonne chance, chérie."*

"I think I had my *bonne chance* long ago," Emily whispered.

Nargis had done her best to prepare a repast for them, although it was clear she was not used to cooking for herself, let alone for others, particularly with the limited supplies of fresh produce available to her. The chaplain and Captain Carruthers ate with them, but left shortly after, explaining that they must set off to be back in Bilkhondar city by nightfall. They refused an offer of overnight accommodation, as Colonel Smythe had made a point of their absence not being prolonged so as to be noticeable.

The Prince himself escorted them from the premises, after which he did not return to the room. Emily was suddenly weary.

"Come, *chérie*," Simone said sympathetically, "it has been a long day for you. Nargis has drawn you a bath."

The bathroom was not opulent by the standards of her splendid apartments in the harem, but it was clean, and the water was hot. Helped by Simone, Emily divested herself of the riding habit, and the European underpinnings which went with it. "I shall never wear those again," she said firmly. "Simone, while I bathe, ask Margis if she has a sari I can borrow."

Simone was back in no time, with a selection of three saris, not loaned, but given, by a delighted Nargis. Emily chose one of palest blue shot with threads of silver, and with skilful hands wrapped the folds of fabric round her slim body. Then she took out the pins from her hair, shook it free, and brushed it carefully and deliberately, until every curl was gone. She wore no jewellery but the silver ring Dara had given her in the harem, and the broad gold band he had slipped on her finger that afternoon.

Simone looked at her, and shook her head gently.

"You have cut off your retreat," she said. "There is now nowhere for you to go."

"I know. But there never was. My choice was made months ago, and I stand by it."

Simone shrugged. "Passion I understand, flirtation I understand, but not this," she said. "Perhaps it is as well that love is not for all of us."

Nargis had made a special effort with the bedroom, which she had decorated with vases of foliage from the garden. There were few actual flowers, for without careful cultivation, little would grow at this height of its own accord, but the greenery was effective, and the kind thought brought tears to Emily's eyes.

A slight movement behind her caught her attention, and she turned to see him standing in the doorway, regarding her pensively.

"Believe me, Emily," he said, "I did not want it to be like this."

It was the first serious, heartfelt statement he had made to her since her arrival, and she thought carefully before replying.

"How often can things be as we plan them? You and should be only too aware that they seldom can. Bu need it make any difference?"

"I think it must," he said. "It matters that I have been deprived – not merely of a throne, that would not have signified – but of a purpose, of the right to play an active part in my country's destiny. It matters that my father is dead, and Bilkhondar in ruins. But what matters most of all is that you should have been brought here, away from a comfortable existence amongst your own people, to live in this cheerless place, found in marriage to a man with no future. I am not sure, Emily, whether I am your prisoner or you are mine."

"I am not concerned with comfort," she told him steadily, "and I found little in common with my 'own people' as you call them. Grieve for your father, for Bilkhondar, but not for me. I did what I chose to do."

He said, "You are, without doubt, a woman in a million," and closing the door softly, left her on her own; they spent the night, these once passionate lovers, in separate rooms. For Emily, it was a night of misery, fighting against feelings of utter despair and rejection.

She told herself forcefully that Dara was not himself, that the balance of his mind had been disturbed by the injuries he had sustained, and his strong sense of personal guilt for his failure to avert Bilkhondar's tragedy. It would have been easier to seek refuge in this hypothesis if he had raved or displayed anger. He was so icily calm and polite, it was difficult to believe him less than perfectly in command of himself. Only the memory of the man he had once been helped her to remain convinced.

It was very easy for someone as shrewd and experienced as Simone to cast a glance at the bedroom and its restrained and silent occupant, and draw the correct conclusions.

"Ah, well, what did you expect?" she said, busying herself straightening the silk coverlet on the divan. "He is proud – he would have wanted to offer you marriage freely, not to have been made over to you, to underwrite his good behaviour."

Emily did not stir from her seat; without any truculence in her voice, she said, "So you think I did wrong to accept Colonel Smythe's terms."

"I think you did what any woman in love would do, and he is reacting as any man would," Simone replied. "He believes you have married him out of pity. Can you not convince him otherwise?"

Emily straightened. "I have my pride, too," she said. "Would you have me throw myself at his feet and weep? The very fact that I am here shouts aloud that I love him."

Simone's eyes were thoughtful. "I am not an expert, for all you may consider me worldly. This love of which you speak, and for which you have suffered so much, I have never felt for any man, and doubt that I shall, for it is not in my nature. But remember, *chérie*, how you behaved in the harem when you believed the Prince to be dead. Did you cry and scream? You did not. You were so cold no one could reach you."

"Prince Dara is like that now. He has lost his father, his child, his throne, his life's meaning. When he heard you were in Poona, he probably believed that you had deserted him, too, and although you have come back, remember his world has turned upside-down, and he can be sure of nothing. Jerk him out of this melancholia, *chérie*. Weep all over him, insult him, fight with him, if you must. But do not simply let things be."

For the rest of the day, Emily mulled over what Simone had said, and she had plenty of time, since she saw nothing of her new husband until the evening, when he observed the courtesies of his married state by dining with her. After a silent meal, he moved away from her and stood gazing out into the darkened court-yard.

Emily moistened her lips and said, "I wonder if I could prevail upon Colonel Smythe to have the pianoforte sent to us. It would be a gargantuan task to transport it here, but it would help to pass the time."

"I am sure the Colonel would be willing to do anything to ensure your compliance with his plans," Dara said languidly.

Emily ignored this, and continued implacably, "Or a few books, perhaps. I swear, a woman never had a less diverting honeymoon."

He still had his back to her, so she could not read his expression, but there was an edge to his voice which was new and alert.

"It is not necessary, Emily, to pretend you came here seeking romance."

There was no sound for a moment but the swish of Emily's sari as she crossed the room and stood so close that she could have reached out and touched him.

She said, "I came here seeking a man I once knew, a man who once promised me his love now and always, whatever happened. I did not find him."

He whirled round, and in the flickering light of the lamps she saw his eyes, alive and struggling fiercely with a multiplicity of emotions, and knew that she had reached him. She faced him without fear, he could have killed her for all she cared, because now, at least, a real and tangible current was passing between them, he was seeing her once more as a woman, and the air around them was alive with possibilities.

Reacting with the lightning-swift reflexes of the old Dara, he grasped her wrist with his lean, strong hand, pulled her towards him and kissed her fiercely, almost viciously, on the mouth. Then he pushed her aside, and strode past her, out of the room.

She stood regaining her breath, and savouring her small but significant triumph. From the way he had kissed her, she knew the was not as devoid of emotion as his recent demeanour had suggested; the love they had shared was not dead, only hidden beneath the hard, brittle carapace his mind had grown to conceal the hurt.

The creaking of the heavy outer door told her that she had waited a fraction too long. She ran from the room, and down the gloomy corridor, in time to see Yusuf sliding the heavy bolts back into position.

"Where is the Prince?" she demanded breathlessly.

"He has ridden out on his horse – the one on which you came, with the white markings."

"Alone – at night? But he can't! Didn't you try to prevent him?" Emily gasped.

The man smiled patiently at her, shaking his head.

"It is not for me to prevent His Highness from taking whatever path he chooses," he said. "It is the first time he had been on horseback since he was wounded, and my heart rejoiced to see the way he sprang into the saddle. Now, truly, he must be recovered."

Emily leaned against the door. She had insulted him out of his glacial calm, goaded him into action, and driven him out into danger once more.

"If he is hurt, I shall not forgive myself," she said.

"Do not fear." Yusuf Khan was stolidly comforting. "Both the Prince and his horse know these hills too well. Even in darkness, he will come to no harm."

Emily walked the floor of her room until midnight, trying hard to believe him. Simone brought tea and stayed with her a while, but finally she sent the other girl to bed, preferring to face the waiting alone. At two in the morning, she lay on the bed and rested a little gazing at the ceiling, and it must have been nearing dawn when she dropped asleep.

The air was cool with the freshness of early morning in the hills, when she opened her eyes. It was full daylight, but infinitely quiet and peaceful. Her eyes strayed around the room, and before she had time to remember the fears of the night, she saw him, standing at the foot of the bed, so still he might have been carved from stone.

"So you're back," she said, unable to hide her smile of relief. Now, before she was sufficiently awake to erect the defensive walls of pride and reserve around her, love shone clear from her pale face, surrounded by the loose, tousled hair.

He said, "Is it true that in Poona you tried to take your own life?"

"Who told you that?" she asked dreamily. "It must have been Simone, I suppose. But I sent her to bed."

"And I have sent her back there again, but not before she had her chance to upbraid me when I came in, as she had been waiting up all night to do. But tell me – is it true?"

She smiled again, and sighed. "It was a clumsy attempt, and they interrupted me before I had the chance, but yes, it is true. I think I was a little crazed, and you see, I thought you were dead."

He knelt by the bed, and took her hand. "You did that for love of me?" he said. "Tell me, how have you borne the way I have behaved towards you since your arrival here, my dearest Emily, my love?"

His eyes, the timbre of his voice, the touch of his hand, all these belonged to the Dara she had known and loved in the past, not to the icy stranger she had married yesterday. She could not speak, so immense was her joy and relief. He lifted her hand and saw the silver ring he had given her that day in the harem, that now seemed so long ago.

"If there be paradise on earth . . ." he said.

"There is," breathed Emily, once again in his arms, but today not a mere harem woman, but his wife, now and for always. "Oh, my love, there is!"

Later, lying side by side, watching the sun light up the garden and pick up the colours of their room, they talked of the past and of the future.

"I seemed to be in a dark tunnel with no light at the end," he said. "For many days I was more or less unconscious, and when I came round, it was to the realisation that I had failed in what I had tried to do, that my worse fears for Bilkhondar had been realised."

"There was not a chance in a million that you could have succeeded," she said. "You must not go on blaming yourself."

"I think I have accepted that, now. Perhaps I knew it at the time, although I had to take that chance in a million. I could not throw in my lot with my father and the Nana Sahib, and the others, who thought this the ideal opportunity to deal the British a body blow. To me, it was all too obvious how they would react."

"You were right." Quietly and without exaggeration, she told him about the night the men of the Deccan Rifles invaded the harem, the death of Qadir Bibi Bano and the behaviour of Major Hargreaves. He listened gravely.

"Some of this I already knew, although not in such detail," he said. "When they told me you had gone to Poona, Emily, I believed that was the end, that I should never see you again. What did life hold for me, but emptiness and futility? I wished I had died in the battle."

"To go to Poona was not my choice," she told him

"Colonel Smythe sent me, much against my wishes. But I thought you were dead, and nothing mattered very much, so I agreed to go. I hated every minute of it, although Mrs. Smythe was so kind to me, and it was wonderful beyond belief to come back here. And then, to discover you were alive!" Her eyes shone as she recalled that dramatic moment. "Dara, how could you be such a fool as to believe I had married you out of pity? All the luxury, the jewels, the fine clothes, the easy living – none of these mean anything to me, compared to this, to the bliss of actually being your wife. I would have married you had you been reduced to begging in the streets of Bilkhondar."

He raised himself on one elbow and looked down at her, the light of humour and interest back in his fine eyes.

"Which I am not. I am rich enough to support you in reasonable style for the rest of our lives," he said. "The British may keep their stipend, we shall not require it."

"But my love, they now have possession of everything in Bilkhondar," she said gently, puzzled.

"I know, but when I was in Europe, my father, who had no idea of how frugally a student at Oxford can live, had large sums of money sent regularly for my requirements. Most of it is still there, in various European banks, a veritable fortune. We shall make this place a small oasis of beauty and comfort. The garden shall be cleared and cultivated, servants will be engaged. You shall have your books and pianoforte," he said teasingly, "in readiness for the day when you no longer find me diverting."

Emily blushed.

"I am sure that day will never come," she declared. "But what will you do, Dara, up here in this isolated place? That is what worries me."

"I did a lot of hard thinking while I was riding last night," he said. "I thought that I could not live for ever without a purpose to my life, and I thought that maybe, sometime in the future, when India is quiet again, and the wounds have healed over a little, there might once more be a role for me in Bilkhondar's destiny. Or for our children, Emily, for you and I are building a bridge to the future, a new world. In the meantime, it occurred to me that no one has yet written a definitive history of Bilkhondar, and here is several years' work for someone with the time and the energy."

He turned to her once more, his eyes bright with love.

"Oh, but that is for the future. For now, I cannot think of anything but you, whom I thought I had lost for ever, here in my arms once again." He kissed her eyes, her lips, her throat, gently at first and then with increasing passion, and, drowning in joy, Emily gave herself up completely to the wonder of this love for which they had both suffered and endured so much. Lost in each other, they let the rest of the world slip away.

And then he slept, peacefully and contentedly, with his head against her breast, a strand of her golden hair falling unheeded across his face. Emily did not sleep - she was too full of emotion. She lay quietly watching the sun bringing back the daylight to the room, listening to the splashing of the old fountain in the garden outside which seemed to echo her faith in their happiness. The past, with its dangers and its delights, was behind them, the future, still a mystery, lay ahead. In this brief moment, suspended between the two, Emily was content.

Masquerade
Historical Romances

Intrigue excitement romance

Don't miss
October's
other enthralling Historical Romance Title

RUNAWAY MAID
by Ann Edgeworth

Miss Robina Westerley is in disgrace again. And this time it is serious. Emphatically refusing Sir Joseph Varley, the suitor of her parents' choice, she takes her destiny into her own hands — and runs away.

Her bright eyes and impulsive spirit lead her into all sorts of predicaments, but with the aid of various devoted helpers, she always manages to escape the worst consequences. More and more often, rescue seems to come from the lofty, imperturbable Sir Giles Gilmore. Yet how can they ever mean anything to each other, when it is so evident that he is going to marry an heiress who can boast immense wealth as well as beauty?

You can obtain this title today from your local paperback retailer

Masquerade
Historical Romances

Intrigue
excitement
romance

THE ABDUCTED HEIRESS
by Jasmine Cresswell

Georgiana Thayne was so determined not to be
married for her money that she pretended to be plain
and childishly stupid. It took an abduction by the
wicked Marquis of Graydon to make her show her
true colours . . .

THE MARKED MAN
by Meriol Trevor

Claudine looked like an innocent schoolgirl, but she
was prepared to shelter Gabriel — the infamous Marked
Man — from the French Revolutionary soldiers who
had invaded her beloved Luxembourg. She soon found
that her heart was in greater danger than her life.

Look out for these titles in your local paperback shop from
9th November 1979

Masquerade
Historical Romances

Intrigue excitement romance

THE EMPEROR'S JEWEL
by Lisa Montague

How could Sophie — Napoleon Bonaparte's beloved ward, the Emperor's Jewel — fall in love with Edmund Apsley, an English spy? It was unthinkable, but it was true.

BLACK FOX
by Kate Buchan

A king's word can create an alliance — but not love, and Isabel Douglass is determined to escape an arranged marriage with the fierce, proud Master of Glencarnie who regards her with open contempt as a mere political pawn. Yet a Fate stronger than either seems to draw them inexorably together . . .

SWEET WIND OF MORNING
by Belinda Grey

Catherine did not want to marry anyone but her childhood sweetheart, Will — certainly not the dark intruder from Queen Elizabeth's court, Sir Piers Tregarron. But Sir Piers, it seemed, did not care what Catherine wanted.

All these titles are still available through your local paperbac retailer.